THE
RED BADGE OF
COURAGE

THE RED BADGE OF COURAGE

An Episode of the American Civil War
&
"The Veteran"

Stephen Crane

With an Introduction by
Shelby Foote

THE MODERN LIBRARY

NEW YORK

2000 Modern Library Paperback Edition

Introduction copyright © 1993 by Shelby Foote

Grateful acknowledgment is made to the following for permission to
reprint previously published material:

CROWN PUBLISHERS, A DIVISION OF RANDOM HOUSE, INC.:
Introduction by Ernest Hemingway from *Men at War: The Best War
Stories of All Time,* edited by Ernest Hemingway. Copyright © 1942
by Crown Publishers, Inc. Reprinted by permission of Crown
Publishers, a division of Random House, Inc.

DOUBLEDAY, A DIVISION OF RANDOM HOUSE, INC., AND MESSRS.
WALKER MARTINEAU ON BEHALF OF THE TRUSTEES OF THE JOSEPH
CONRAD ESTATE: Excerpt from "His War Book" from *Last Essays* by
Joseph Conrad. Copyright © 1926 by Doubleday, a division of
Random House, Inc. Rights outside of the United States are
controlled by the Trustees of the Joseph Conrad Estate, administered
by Messrs. Walker Martineau. Reprinted by permission of
Doubleday, a division of Random House, Inc., and Messrs. Walker
Martineau on behalf of the Trustees of the Joseph Conrad Estate.

NEW YORK UNIVERSITY PRESS: Excerpt from a letter by Stephen
Crane to John N. Hilliard from *Stephen Crane: Letters* edited by
R. W. Stallman and Lillian Gilkes. Reprinted by permission of New
York University Press.

LIBRARY OF CONGRESS CATALOGING-IN-PUBLICATION DATA
Crane, Stephen, 1871–1900.
The red badge of courage: an episode of the American Civil War/Stephen
Crane; with an introduction by Shelby Foote.—2000 Modern
Library pbk. ed.
p.   cm.
Includes bibliographical references.
ISBN 0-679-78320-2
1. United States—History—Civil War, 1861–1865—Fiction.
2. Chancellorsville (Va.), Battle of, 1863—Fiction. I. Title.
PS1449.C85 R3   2000
813´.4—dc21   00-37093

Modern Library website address: www.modernlibrary.com

Printed in the United States of America

2 4 6 8 9 7 5 3 1

STEPHEN CRANE

Stephen Townley Crane, the iconoclastic novelist, poet, short-story writer, journalist, and war correspondent who propelled American literature into the modernist age, was born in Newark, New Jersey, on November 1, 1871. The origins of his genius will perhaps always remain elusive: he was of the opinion that "writing was a business like any other" and believed that "one could train one's mind to observe and a man should be able to say something worthwhile about any event." Crane's tragically abbreviated career, which spanned less than ten years, dates from 1892, when the New York *Tribune* printed the novice reporter's so-called Sullivan County sketches, a series of rustic stories set in the New York countryside. His first novel, *Maggie: A Girl of the Streets,* was privately printed in 1893 and broke new ground with its realistic portrait of life in the slums of New York City. *The Black Riders,* a volume of poetry, came out in 1895.

Crane's next book, *The Red Badge of Courage,* brought him international fame when it was published in October 1895. "*The Red Badge of Courage* has long been considered the first great 'modern' novel of war by an American—the first novel of literary distinction to present war without heroics and this in a spirit of total irony and skepticism," wrote Alfred Kazin. "What makes [it] so remarkable, and a pioneer in the literature of war, is that it was written entirely from instinct by a young newspaperman in his early twenties who had never seen a war." "With *The Red Badge of Courage,* Crane burst upon the American public with the effect of a Civil War projectile lain dormant beneath a city square for thirty years," observed Ralph Ellison. "That *The Red Badge* was widely read during Crane's own time was a triumph of his art."

Afterward Crane led a vagabond existence as a journalist and war correspondent while continuing to write fiction. Capitalizing on the success of *The Red Badge of Courage,* he turned out *The Little Regiment* (1896), a collection of Civil War stories. In addition he completed two more novels: *George's Mother* (1896), a second Bowery tale often viewed as a companion volume to *Maggie,* and *The Third Violet* (1897), a portrait of bohemian life that is generally considered his least accomplished work. Crane's earlier travels in Mexico and the American Southwest inspired two of his most famous short stories, "The Bride Comes to Yellow Sky" (1897) and "The Blue Hotel" (1898). His harrowing misadventures at sea en route to Cuba resulted in "The Open Boat" (1897), a story many critics regard as his masterpiece. In 1899, the final year of his life, Crane published *War Is Kind,* a second book of verse; *Active Service,* an adventure-romance based on his experiences as a reporter in the Greco-Turkish War; and *The Monster and Other Stories,* whose disturbing title story provides a sharp study of community malice.

Stephen Crane suffered a series of tubercular hemorrhages while living in England during the spring of 1900 and died in a sanatorium in Badenweiler, Germany, on June 5, 1900. Several of Crane's last works were issued posthumously, including *Whilomville Stories* (1900), a volume of tales about small-town America; *Wounds in the Rain* (1900), a collection of short stories drawn from his exploits in the Spanish-American War; *Great Battles of the World* (1901), a work of nonfiction culled from a popular magazine series; *Last Words* (1902), a miscellany of articles, stories, and newspaper sketches; and *The O'Ruddy* (1903), a swashbuckling Irish romance left unfinished at the time of his death.

"Crane in his short life quickly showed himself the most original, most ruthlessly independent, most sardonic novelist of his talented generation," judged Alfred Kazin. "Nowhere in American writing was a godless world expressed with so much terseness and finality as in the work of Stephen Crane." The poet John Berryman, one of Crane's most celebrated biographers, concluded: "Crane was perhaps as original as an artist can be, and be valuable. . . . By a margin he is probably the greatest American story-writer, he stands as an artist not far below Hawthorne and James, he is one of our few poets, and one of the few manifest geniuses the country has produced."

CONTENTS

INTRODUCTION

Shelby Foote

Stephen Crane's *Red Badge*, having reached its centennial, fulfills the academic dictum requiring a shelf life of one hundred years to establish a book as a classic. Not that it needs such pious substantiation. No American novel, neither *The Scarlet Letter* nor *Moby Dick*, not even *Huckleberry Finn*, has a stronger claim to membership in that sifted category, and this began to be recognized almost from the start, first abroad—as was earlier the case with the speeches of Abraham Lincoln and later with the novels of William Faulkner—and then, by rebound, on this side of the ocean. Ernest Hemingway, for example, midway through that qualifying span, after referring to it rather slightingly as a "boy's dream of war," added at once that *The Red Badge of Courage* was "truer to how war was than any war the boy who wrote it would ever live to see," and finally, having taken what he had learned from Crane to heart in his own work, pronounced it "one of the finest books of our literature."

Conceived as "a pot-boiler, something that would take the boarding school element," the first draft was written, Crane said, in "ten nights" during the early spring of 1893, four or five months past his twenty-first birthday in November. Like other writers before and since, Crane looked at what he had done and saw that he had a good deal more on his hands than he had intended or even suspected at the outset; "so I must do it all over again, I guess," he told a friend on April 2, and presently did just that, lengthening and converting it—still in rough draft, subject to further expansions and contractions—into more or less the classic we know today. Getting it published was of course another matter, as he knew from previous experience with his first book, a shorter work originally called "A Girl of the Streets, A Story of New York," but later titled *Maggie: A Girl of the Streets*.

Still earlier, a double college dropout, he had worked as a free-lance journalist and sometime stringer for the New York *Tribune*, contributing sketches of rural life in Sullivan County, New York, and the resort goings-on at Asbury Park, New Jersey, where—fourteenth of fourteen brothers and sisters, nine of whom survived infancy and seven of whom survived him—he had lived with his mother since the death of his Methodist minister father ten years before. His schooling during this decade, ten to twenty, included two years at a military boarding school in Claverack, New York, where he made cadet captain, and brief stays at Lafayette College and Syracuse University, where he paid little attention to his studies and mainly divided his time between his Delta Upsilon fraternity house, with particular attention to billiards and poker, and the baseball diamond and the football gridiron. Soon after he dropped out ("to recover from college," he explained) he took to staying with East Side artist friends across the Hudson and exploring the tenements and flophouses, the saloons and music halls of the Bowery, which he pronounced "the most interesting place in New York." Previously he had displayed a certain facility in his newspaper sketches, a flipness that attracted editors and readers; but now his exposure to the seamy tumult of the Bowery, along with his scattered reading of the new "naturalist" novels and the pulps of the avant-garde, occasioned and urged a change of purpose and manner in his writing. "If I had kept to my clever Rudyard-Kipling style, the road might have been shorter," he afterwards declared, "but, ah, it wouldn't be the true road."

As it turned out, the road was short in any case— some eight or nine years, all told, including the apprenticeship—and extraordinarily bumpy from the start. *Maggie* was a Bowery tale, with all the attendant miseries and vices, written in accordance with Crane's definition of the novel as "a succession of sharply outlined pictures which pass before the reader like a panorama, having each its definite impression." Maggie herself, who "blossomed in a mud puddle," works first as a seamstress in a collar-and-cuffs sweatshop, is seduced, turns streetwalker ("a girl of the painted cohorts of the city"), and winds up throwing herself into the "deathly black" East River. Hackneyed in plot, the novel was far from hackneyed in the writer's treatment of that plot or the people who moved through it, attended neither by authorial condemnation nor by apparent compassion. Many of the "impressions" along the way were all too "definite" for the editors to whom the manuscript was submitted. Almost without exception they reacted as if the frail young man in his shabby clothes had tossed a dead rat, or even a live one, on their desks. They wanted no part of it, and were quick to say so. Their main complaint, however, that the work contained "no visible sentiment," was taken by Crane as a compliment. "Sentiment is the devil" was at the core of his belief.

So he turned elsewhere. Cashing in some coal-mining stock he had inherited from his mother the year before, he paid $869 to have 1,100 paperback copies of *Maggie* printed by a lower Sixth Avenue firm specializing in medical books and religious tracts. Later informed that he had been overcharged by $700, he accepted this "as proffered evidence of my imbecility." Further testimony to his commercial incompetence lay in the fact that, at fifty cents a copy, a complete sellout would have left him worse than $300 in the hole—proof enough, if proof was needed, that it wasn't primarily money he was after; it was fame. All the same, taking his cue from the printing company, which was careful not to have its name appear on the mustard-yellow cover, and from an editor friend who warned that the book might "bring on you a storm of controversy," Crane decided to use the screen of a pseudonym, and after selecting Johnson and Smith as "the stupidest names in the world," set-

tled on Johnston Smith as his nom de plume, adding
the *t* to Johnson to give it, after all, a touch of class.
Besides, the name would only be temporary, pending
the elevation of the book to the heights of bestseller-
dom and critical acclaim. As he put it afterwards,
looking somewhat ruefully back, "I was going to wait
until the world was pyrotechnic about *Maggie* and
then I was going to flop down like a trapeze per-
former from a wire, and coming forward with all the
modest grace of a consumptive nun, say, I am he,
friends."

No such acrobatics were called for. Despite the encouragement of Hamlin Garland, who was ten years
Crane's senior and whose *Main-Travelled Roads* had
appeared two years before, and the active support of
William Dean Howells, author of *Silas Lapham* and
other novels, recent editor of the *Atlantic Monthly*,
and at forty-five already the dean of American letters—"realists" both, acknowledged by Crane as his
mentors—the work received little attention from reviewers or potential customers. In part this was the
result of some confusion for the few who ventured to
look inside the novel's ugly covers. There seemed to
be two Johnston Smiths, one old-style, at times griev-
ously awkward, and the other insufferably new. One
wrote, "Down the avenue came boastfully sauntering
a lad of sixteen years, although the chronic sneer of
an ideal manhood already sat upon his lips." Explana-
tions later devised to account for such passages identified them as parody; this was, after all, what became

known as the Mauve Decade, and Crane was mocking the overwrought style of his period even as he reflected it. The other Smith, mainly evident in dialogue portions of the book, had Maggie's seducer remark, "Say, Mag, I'm stuck on yer shape. It's outa sight." If this was startling to readers, nearly half a century before the emergence of Clifford Odets on Broadway, other bits were even more so. "Deh moon looks like hell, don't it?" Maggie's younger brother says reverently, gazing upward.

Whatever the cause, including the fear of being charged with peddling pornography, booksellers refused to handle the thing at all. Brentano's, the rare exception, took a dozen copies on Howells' recommendation, sold two, and returned the unsold ten, which were added to the stack of unwanted others propped against one wall of Crane's rented room to serve as a seat for visitors. "Well," he said, by way of consolation, "at least I've done something. I wrote a book."

In point of fact, by that time—March of 1893—he was at work on two more books. One was another Bowery novel, whose original title, "A Woman Without Weapons," was soon changed to *George's Mother*. Work on it was interrupted, at about the time that Maggie hit (or failed to hit) the stands, by the ten-night spurt that produced the first draft of *The Red Badge*, whose working title was "Private Fleming, His Various Battles." Like most young men of his time, he had listened to veterans tell tales of their Civil War experiences, a generation back, and in his boyhood had read articles, nearly all of them by men of rank, in stray copies of the *Century Illustrated Magazine,* collected and published five years before in an outsized four-volume set called *Battles and Leaders of the Civil War,* complete with photographs, drawings, and maps. Historians and buffs prized the work as a primary source and quoted it liberally— as they still do—in and out of footnotes. Crane borrowed a set, read it selectively, and found himself disturbed, not so much by what was in it, but rather by what was not. "I wonder that *some* of these fellows don't tell how it *felt* in those scrapes," he complained.

Omitting most of what they included, and including much of what they left out, he had struck the note he wanted in the preliminary draft, but he saw that a great deal remained to be done before it measured up to all that he wanted it to become. Steady work on the rewriting was delayed, however, by having to turn out a series of newspaper pieces, still about life in the Tenderloin, which barely earned him the little money he needed to live there, but which he hoped to see collected someday, along with others, in a book to be called "Midnight Sketches." Then in June he decamped to visit two of his brothers, one across the Hudson at Lake View (since absorbed by Paterson) and the other at Port Jervis, New York, up on the Delaware River near the New Jersey and Pennsylvania lines. Both were rural retreats and provided a near-idyllic four-month interlude in which he divided his time between tennis and football, a bevy of admiring nieces, and extensive, intensive revision of his war novel.

In October he came back to the city, settled in much as before, and continued to peg away at the manuscript, past his twenty-second birthday, on through Christmas and New Year's, then apparently put it aside to cool and turned again to journalism, producing in January and February two of his best pieces, "An Experiment in Misery" and "The Men in the Storm," one about a night in a flophouse, which he described as "a graveyard, where bodies are merely flung," the other about a breadline, where men stand in line before a Bowery mission, hunched against the terrible 1894 blizzard, waiting "upon the threshold of their hopes." There were signs here of something else he had been up to: poetry—though he did not call his verses poems; he called them "lines," and indeed that was what they were, unrhymed, unmetered, untitled, and sometimes unfathomable on short acquaintance. However, when Crane brought Hamlin Garland a sheaf of them to read in early March, Garland admired them and encouraged him to submit them for publication without delay. Asked how they came to be written, Crane pointed to his temple and replied, "I've got five or six all in a little row up here." Incredulous, Garland took him up on that. "Do one for me," he said. Crane did, then and there at Garland's desk, and Garland later said that "one of his most powerful

poems . . . flowed from his pen like oil." Perhaps it
was the one about "a man who lived a life of fire":

> This life glowed,
> A dire red stain, indelible;
> Yet when he was dead
> He saw that he had not lived.

In mid-April Crane was back again, clutching another sheaf of papers. Garland supposed he had
brought him more poems to read, but when he
opened the rather dog-eared manuscript he saw that it
was prose and was headed "Private Fleming, His Various Battles." As he read—"The first sentence fairly
took me captive," he later wrote—his excitement
grew; he "experienced the thrill of the editor who has
fallen unexpectedly upon the work of a genius."
When in time he reached the final handwritten sheet,
his spirits took a drop. "Where's the rest of it?" he
said. Embarrassed, Crane explained that a typist was
holding the second half in hock for his $15 fee. Gar-
land lent him the money on condition that he would
return next day with the rest of the book. When he
did, Garland read it with continued admiration and
declared that it should be submitted at once for publication. Before leaving for Chicago in late April he
wrote a strong letter of recommendation for Crane
to take, along with the typescript, to S. S. McClure,
there in New York.

In early May, having done so, Crane heard from

the publisher that the novel—now permanently titled *The Red Badge of Courage. An Episode of the American Civil War*—was altogether acceptable and was being held pending a decision whether to release it through his newspaper syndicate or run it as a serial in his widely distributed magazine, *McClure's*. Delighted that he was about to be launched at last, Crane took up *George's Mother* where he had left off, about that time a year before, and passed the word to Garland that he was "eat[ing] with charming regularity at least twice a day. I am content," he added, "and am writing another novel which is a bird." His cup fairly ran over before the end of the month, when he heard from the Boston publishers Copeland and Day, to whom he had sent some seventy of his elliptical poems, that they planned to bring them out in a book, perhaps by the end of the year.

Still on the previous year's schedule, he left the city for his brother's house at Hartwood, up in hilly Sullivan County, for sustained work on the novel he called "a bird." Though he was interrupted from time to time by assignments from the muckracking McClure, including pieces as diverse as one on "Coney Island's Failing Days" and another on conditions in some Pennsylvania coal mines, mainly he plugged away at *George's Mother* and was "content," on through the summer and into fall. But there were other, more irritating distractions. Copeland and Day, for instance, wanted to exclude certain poems from the collection, on grounds that they were blasphemous or anarchic.

Crane refused to go along. "It is the anarchy which I particularly insist upon," he told them. A graver problem was McClure, who, nagged by the notion that the Civil War had been exhausted as a popular subject for fiction, kept delaying the decision he had begun to ponder in early May.

Back in New York by October, Crane wrote to Garland in mid-November, announcing that he had wound up *George's Mother*—which, he exulted, "leaves *Maggie* at the post"—and had taken another decisive step by retrieving his *Red Badge* typescript. "McClure was a Beast about the war novel," he declared. "He kept it for six months until I was near mad."

By way of an upshot he submitted the reclaimed work to Irving Bacheller, partner in a rival newspaper syndicate. Unlike McClure, Bacheller not only knew a good thing when he saw it, he was also willing to take chances. He read it overnight and sent for Crane next morning to inform him of a plan to offer his clients a cut-down version of the work—18,000 of its 55,000 words, just under one third—for publication in installments of whatever length they chose. The outright price tendered the author, with no royalties or bonuses involved, was ninety dollars, which came to half a cent a word. Crane accepted promptly, anticipating another trapeze descent, this time with no need for coming forward with modest grace to announce that he was he.

As it turned out, the venture was successful beyond his and Bacheller's fondest hopes, and indeed almost beyond belief. The series was scheduled for January production, but the advance sheets met with such enthusiasm from editors, near and far, that the syndicate pulled the release date forward a full month. The first of six installments ran in the *Philadelphia Press* on December 3, along with an editorial saluting the author on the threshold of his fame, and the *New York Press* ran the whole thing in one issue, severely compressed into seven close-set columns, one week later, by which time hundreds of other papers across the country had joined the rush. Crane, just past his twenty-third birthday, was fairly launched. Invited by the Philadelphia editor to come down for a visit, he and Bacheller arrived by train before the month was out, and were given a rousing welcome. "Word flew from cellar to roof that the great Stephen Crane was in the office," a city-room observer wrote. "Editors, reporters, compositors, proofreaders crowded around him shaking his hand. It was a revelation of the commanding power of genius."

Impressed by his find—as well he might be—Bacheller had already hired him to undertake, as a roving reporter, a trip through parts of the West and the South. Crane delayed his departure in order to be at home for New Year's, 1895, and also to read proof on his book of poems, now titled *The Black Riders and Other Lines,* due out in the spring with its dedication "To Hamlin Garland." Something else he did. Emboldened by his new celebrity, he submitted first the newspaper clippings and then the full-length type-script of *The Red Badge* to Ripley Hitchcock of Appleton and Company, a leading New York publisher. He had received no word of acceptance, let alone a contract, when he headed west on the first leg of his Bacheller assignment. "Any news of the war story will be grateful to me," he rather wistfully wrote Hitchcock from Saint Louis at the end of January.

In early February he was in Lincoln, Nebraska, living in a hotel room, eating in cheap restaurants, and hanging around the *State Journal* newspaper office in hope of receiving an overdue check from Bacheller and some word from Hitchcock, and when neither came he turned moody. Eighteen-year-old Willa Cather, a Nebraska State student and part-time staffer for the *Journal*, found him so when they met there. She admired his hands, "long, white, and delicately shaped, with thin, nervous fingers," and his eyes, which were "large and dark and full of lustre and changing lights, but with a profound melancholy always lurking deep in them." Back in December she had copy-read his novel for the paper, and wanting to be a writer herself she looked forward to talking with him. "Oh," he said on their first encounter, noticing a volume of Maupassant on her desk, "you're moping, are you?" Before long, they became friends and he confided to her something of the way he went about practicing his craft. "The detail of a thing has to filter through my blood," he told her, "and then it comes out like a native product. But it takes forever." If this gave her pause, what he added later, in response to a question about the rules for becoming a writer, was even less encouraging. "You can't do it by rule," he said flatly, "any more than you can learn to dance by rule. You have to have the itch of the thing in your fingers, and if you haven't—well, you're damned lucky, and you'll live long and prosper, that's all."

When the syndicate check arrived he traveled westward another hundred-odd miles, interviewing impoverished farmers on the frozen plains—one of whom, asked how he got along without government help, replied, "Don't git along, stranger. Who the hell told you I did get along?" Crane came back to Lincoln to file his story and found waiting for him a letter from Hitchcock accepting *The Red Badge*, with royalties set at 10 percent and no mention of an advance. "I would be glad to have Appleton and Co. publish the story on those terms," he replied laconically, quite as if he had not been waiting on tiptoe all those weeks. "I am going from here to New Orleans. The ms. could be corrected by me there in short order."

Now he set out on a three-month hegira, in the course of which the stories he filed were featured prominently by editors who valued the draw of his byline. An outlander, self-defined as "about as much of a Jerseyman as you can find," he brought a new eye to familiar and unfamiliar scenes that jumped with life from his journalistic pen, and what was more he stored up experiences which, after the filtering process he had described to Cather back in Lincoln, would emerge during the next few years as the best of his, and indeed America's, short fiction. He took the train, by way of Kansas City, to Hot Springs, Arkansas, then on to New Orleans in time for Mardi Gras and final revisions on the typescript of *The Red Badge,* which arrived soon after he did. Returning it to Hitchcock in early March, he was off for Galveston and San Antonio, Texas, then moved on to Laredo and caught the Aztec Limited for Mexico City. All this time he was writing of what he saw and heard and felt; Bacheller was getting his money's worth and more, and so was Crane, whose lifelong love of color reached its peak below the border. "In Mexico the atmosphere seldom softens anything," he wrote. "It devotes its energies to making highlights, bringing everything forward, making colors fairly volcanic."

Life here was exotic and impoverished, flamboyant and drab, and gave his pen full scope in all directions. Popocatepetl made him gasp; he even considered climbing it, until he reconsidered. He acquired a pair of outsized silver spurs—which he said gave him the look of a telegraph lineman and made him sound like a pair of cymbals when he walked—a gaudy serape, and a large nickel-plated Smith & Wesson revolver complete with a low-slung holster, all three of which he kept close by as talismans from then on. His crowning adventure, however, came during an April horseback trip through the back country. He and his native guide took a room for the night in a village cantina and

were awakened by the arrival of the bandito Ramón
Colorado and a number of *compañeros*. There was
drunken talk of killing the yanqui intruder for his
spurs and pistol, but this was delayed by the arrival of
some women, and the party that followed gave Crane
and the guide their chance to slip out of doors before
dawn, saddle and mount their horses, and try for a
getaway in the desert. Chased by the bandits, they
were about to be overtaken when, after the manner of
light fiction, they happened upon a detachment of *ru-
rales,* who drove their pursuers off. When Crane later
wrote about it, in a story called "One Dash—Horses,"
his main praise was for his nimble and determined little pony. All his life he had been fond of horses, and
this one was the hero of the tale.

In early May, rounding out a solid month abroad—
the weather, he said, had given his face "the color of a
brick sidewalk"—he saw an American girl "in a new
spring gown" on the street in Puebla, one in a group
of tourists, and was instantly stricken homesick. "I
ran to the railroad office. I cried: 'What is the shortest
route to New York?' I left Mexico."

Returning on May 16, he found waiting for him
copies of *The Black Riders,* which had come out five
days before. For the first time he held in his hands a
published book with his name on the title page by
way of authentication of his hopes. "When he was
not working," an artist friend from his Bowery days
was to recall, "he would sit writing his name—
Stephen Crane, Stephen Crane, Stephen Crane—on

books, magazines, and loose sheets of paper around the studio." Now there was this fulfillment, with another still to come: Hitchcock informed him that *The Red Badge* was scheduled for publication in October, in time to ride the Christmas-shopping wave.

As he had done for the previous two years, he left the city and thus eased the strain of waiting, all through the summer and into fall, at Port Jervis and Hartwood, where, as he presently reported to friends left behind, he spent his time "cruising around the woods in corduroy and feeling great. I have lots of fun getting healthy," he added, though he could not have had much fun reading some of the reviews of his *Black Riders,* which were mixed at best. Howells had already admitted that he found the poems "too orphic" for his taste, and now a *Tribune* reporter took Crane to task for "futility and affectation" in his so-called "lines," and wound up pronouncing them "so much trash." Others thought better of them and him, referring to their author as "the Aubrey Beardsley of poetry"—there was a drawing of an orchid on the cover, while the poems themselves were printed all in caps—and calling him "a true poet whose verse, long after the eccentricity of its form has worn off, fascinates us and forbids us to lay the volume down until the last line has been read." Crane apparently took such things in his stride, the bad with the good. "I see they are making some stir," he said of the poems in a letter to the publisher, inquiring about sales.

He also got some work done during those corduroy

days, including a Civil War short story, "A Mystery of Heroism," some follow-up Mexico sketches for Bacheller, and the fictionalized "One Dash." By the end of summer he was blocking out a fourth novel. An uncharacteristic courtship tale concerning an impoverished young painter and a vacationing heiress, it was called at first "The Eternal Patience," then later *The Third Violet*. He was about one fifth of the way into its first draft when *The Red Badge of Courage* was published in early October.

Despite the anticipated Christmas rush, sales at first were sluggish. Then the reviews began coming in from all across the country. Mostly they were good; some were practically ecstatic. *The Atlantic Monthly*, for example, pronounced the novel "great enough to start a new fashion in literature," and the *New York Press* took this a long step further. "One should be forever slow in charging an author with genius," the *Press* declared, "but it must be confessed that *The Red Badge of Courage* is open to the suspicion of having greater power and originality than can be girdled by the name of talent." Sales responded to such praise, and Crane himself was delighted—especially with the effect on his brothers and sisters, who had begun to despair of him back in his dropout days. "Gee!" he wrote from Hartwood to a friend in the city. "I simply can't go around to see 'em near enough. It's great. I am no longer a black sheep but a star."

He was indeed, and the star shone brighter still when word arrived of the reaction in England, where the book came out in November, six weeks after the American edition, and touched off what H. G. Wells would call an "orgy of praise." George Wyndham, undersecretary of state for war in Her Majesty's Government, referred to Crane, in the first paragraph of a lengthy explication in the high-toned London *New Review,* as "a great artist with something new to say and, consequently, with a new way of saying it," and praised his descriptions of battle for being "more complete than Tolstoï's, more true than Zola's." Another British reviewer declared that the novel gave him "the feeling of being pelted from different directions by hail—hail that is hot." Joseph Conrad and Ford Madox Hueffer joined the chorus, alongside Wells. Yet the most effective support from that direction, at any rate with regard to sales and the growth of the young author's popular reputation, came from a fellow American, Harold Frederic, himself a novelist and London correspondent for the *New York Times.* In January he informed his stateside readers of the excitement the work had stirred up in literary Britain. Readers there, he said, had found it "more vehemently alive and heaving with dramatic human action than any other book of our times." Pressing the point to expand it, he added fervently that *The Red Badge* was "one of those deathless books which must be read by everybody who desires to be, or to seem, a connoisseur of modern fiction. If there were in existence any books of similar character, one could start confidently by saying that it was the best of its kind. But it is a book outside of all classifications."

Bookshops took note, and soon the novel was selling briskly all across both countries. By early spring Appleton was printing a fourth edition, and a ninth would be out in the early fall, by which time the "orphic" *Black Riders,* pulled along in its wake, had achieved an incredible sixth edition. Crane at first enjoyed his new fame, though at a cautious distance up in Sullivan County, except for a pre-Christmas trip to Buffalo for a testimonial dinner sponsored by Elbert Hubbard's Philistine Society; Hubbard—"a clever-looking duck," Crane called him—was adept at blowing his own horn and was sometimes willing to blow another's, if only by way of swelling the din. Leading editors from around the state, as well as from Boston, Washington, Denver, and New Orleans, raised their glasses in toasts, and Crane, boylike in a borrowed dinner jacket, even managed to respond. He seemed to weather the joshing along with the praise—"If he never produces another thing," Hubbard would soon be saying of Crane and his *Badge,* "he has done enough to save the fag end of the century from literary disgrace"—but the honoree returned to Hartwood feeling that he had somehow been used, as indeed he had.

Besides, publishers were after him for stories and sketches, most of them having to do with battle, and though he agreed to do one for McClure, a story titled "The Little Regiment," he found it hard. "I have invented the sum of my invention in regard to war," he confessed, "and this story keeps me in internal despair." In a year-end note to Hitchcock, accompanying the swiftly completed manuscript of *The Third Violet*, he extended this confession: "It's pretty rotten work. I used myself up on the accursed 'Red Badge.'" Hitchcock seemed to agree in a reply suggesting a rewrite of the courtship novel. But Crane wanted no part of the task, saying, "People may just as well discover now that the high dramatic key of *The Red Badge* cannot be sustained."

All the same, when Frederic's *Times* review arrived from London, along with Wyndham's spun-out paean and the news that his book was all the rage over there, he ventured into New York toward the end of January to hear firsthand all that was going on in that direction. He soon found out. Not only was he besieged by admiring strangers who gushed and demanded autographs, he also found that some old friends now looked at him with unwelcome awe. What was worse, he fell among intellectuals. "They stand me against walls with a teacup in my hand," he later protested, "and tell me how I have stolen all my things from de Maupassant, Zola, Loti, and the bloke who wrote—I forgot the name." The result was panic. Without taking time to cancel appointments, he fled posthaste back to Hartwood. "I couldn't breathe in that accursed tumult," he explained by mail to a friend left behind in the city. "On Friday it had me keyed to a point where I was no more than a

wild beast and I had to make a dash for it willy-nilly."
Apologizing to Hitchcock for having missed a scheduled conference, he declared: "I had grown used to
being called a damned ass but this sudden new admiration of my friends has made a gibbering idiot of
me. I shall stick to my hills."

When I first encountered *The Red Badge,* back in my
early teens, it fairly bowled me over, this story of how
a New York farmboy who, in his terrifying baptism of
fire—a baptism of which it could truly be said, in
churchly terms, that it was "by total immersion"—
first turns tail and runs, a coward, but then rejoins his
regiment and comports himself, throughout the second day of battle, as a hero. More than half a century
later, and with my own war behind me, the novel
bowls me over still, but in a different way, especially
in my understanding of Crane's ultimate assessment
of his young protagonist: "He was a man."

From the time of that furious ten-night burst of
first-draft writing, in the early spring of 1893, to the
presumably final product in New Orleans, in March
of 1895, he had tinkered with and labored over the
text, off and on, for two full years. Like Schliemann
at Troy, explicators have unearthed at least seven lay-
ers of composition and revision underlying the version most of us read today, although some of those
scholars—ignoring the fact that Crane never expressed any reservations about what he had passed for
the printer—restore the excised portions, long and

short, in brackets or in supplements, in an attempt to reinforce their notion of what it was that Crane had been trying to say before he yielded to pressure from Ripley Hitchcock to clip the soaring novel's wings; which, incidentally, is rather like copping the old plea, "The devil made me do it." Crane didn't believe in the devil, nor in "the lake of fire and the rest of the sideshows," and would probably be no more than mildly interested in the outcome. He had known what he was after from the start, yet it was only by making the effort, including the additions and excisions, that he discovered how to get where he was going. The point is that he got there, and he got there in the fewest possible words.

From the outset, having chosen his model—Chancellorsville, as even the most elementary student of the conflict can plainly see from point to point in Crane's account—he was determined to make it universal, not only to broaden its scope but also to avoid the harping of veterans and those who would presently be called buffs. "I evaded them," he afterwards explained, "because it was essential that I should make my battle a type and name no names." Only two place-names are mentioned throughout, Washington and Richmond, and one river, the Rappahannock. Except for the subtitle, added later, not even the war itself is identified. Neither secession nor emancipation is referred to, any more than are Abraham Lincoln and Jefferson Davis; Joe Hooker is never spotted through the drifting smoke, astride his big white horse, and no rumor makes the rounds to tell of Stonewall Jackson's fatal wounding in the flame-stitched twilight of the first day's fighting. In the course of Crane's revisions, even the main characters' names—Jim Conklin, Wilson, and Henry Fleming—were deleted, outside of dialogue passages, and changed respectively to "the tall soldier," "the loud soldier," and "the youth," whose surname remains undisclosed until midway through the book, when he imagines his comrades jeering at his absence, "Where's Henry Fleming? He run, didn't 'e? Oh, my." Not that this avoidance of the nominal specific detracts from the verisimilitude of the novel in its depiction of combat; quite the opposite, in fact. "I was with Crane at Antietam," a retired veteran colonel proudly claimed soon after the book appeared.

For the most part, this triumph of conviction proceeds from the writing itself. If *The Red Badge* has a hero, surely that hero is the American language, and yet the major literary influence on Crane in his use of that instrument came from abroad, from France by way of Russia: first from Stendhal, whose *Charterhouse of Parma* has its young protagonist, Fabrizio del Dongo, flounder about on the field of Waterloo in a state of disoriented confusion much like Henry Fleming's. Crane, it seems, had never read Stendhal, but Tolstoy had, and had learned from him, and Crane learned from Tolstoy, whose *Sebastopol* came out in translation half a dozen years before the first draft of

The Red Badge was put on paper. Crane had read and admired it, but apparently not *War and Peace* ("It goes on and on like Texas," he is reported to have complained) nor Zola's *La Débâcle*, also often cited as an influence, though Crane himself only said of him, "I find him pretty tiresome." In a larger sense his major influences came from life itself, from the people he knew and moved among and the veterans he talked with. For example, "I believe that I got my sense of the rage of conflict on the football field," he once declared, and his Claverack training in close-order drill and the manual of arms was of greater use to him than anyone trying to write about army life without such training could ever know.

Impressionist or expressionist, realist or naturalist—he was called all those things and more—he did have a credo he stuck to from the start. A preacher's son, he said flatly: "Preaching is fatal to art in literature. I try to give readers a slice out of life, and if there is any moral or lesson in it I do not point it out. I let the reader find it for himself." All unknown, he was combining Emily Dickinson's "Tell all the truth but tell it slant" with John Keats's "negative capability" when he wrote, late in his short life, "An artist, I think, is nothing but a powerful memory that can move itself at will through certain experiences sideways, and every artist must be in some things powerless as a dead snake."

Working within this credo and definition, he could be wonderfully exact and at the same time highly evocative in communicating sensation, the sight and sound and feel of an action or an object. Of a green command, ordered into its first shoulder-to-shoulder advance under fire, he writes: "The line fell slowly forward like a toppling wall, and, with a convulsive gasp that was intended for a cheer, the regiment began its journey." Up ahead, "The forest made a tremendous objection," and presently, at closer range, "bullets buffed into men" and "grunting bundles of blue began to drop." The attackers bared their teeth as they charged, and "their eyes shone all white." Guyed by veteran units they passed on their withdrawal to the rear, "the men trudged with sudden heaviness, as if they bore upon their bended shoulders the coffin of their honor." Critics might bridle at grammatical lapses and complain that the text fairly bristled with pathetic fallacies— some more pathetic than others—but there could be no denying that what came across in the end had a tactile validity beyond anything of its kind they had encountered in their book-cramped lives. No wonder the old line colonel thought he had fought alongside Crane at Antietam or that other veterans were amazed to learn that the battle he described so well (and from the inside, so to speak, all those thirty years ago) had been fought nearly a decade before he was born.

In time, readers would come to see that there might be more beneath than there was above the novel's surface; reticence was a masking device that magnified even as it concealed. John Berryman, a mid-twentieth-century Crane biographer and poet, speaks in this connection of "the immense power of the tacit"; but Frank

Norris, a contemporary, put it in simpler terms, re-marking that Crane "knew when to shut up." Others who knew him in his life gave other clues. Wells, for example, spoke of his "persistent selection of the ele-ments of an impression." But perhaps the finest as-sessment of all, from Crane's own day to the present, was given by another British contemporary, Edward Garnett, author of "Mr. Stephen Crane: An Appreci-ation," the first in-depth study of his work as a whole, up to the time he knew him in England. Garnett re-vised the piece after Crane's death, adding percep-tively: "It is his irony that checks the emotional intensity of his delineation, and suddenly reveals pas-sion at high tension in the clutch of the implacable tides of life. It is the perfect fusion of these two forces of passion and irony that creates Crane's spiritual background, and raises his work, at its finest, into the higher zone of man's tragic conflict with the universe."

The novel's prevalent irony begins with its title. Henry Fleming's "red badge of courage" is an all but self-inflicted wound, suffered while trying to question one of O. O. Howard's rattled Dutchmen, numbers of whom—skedaddlers too, but faster on their feet, thrown rearward in panic by Jackson's flank attack—had run past him moaning, "Say, where de plank road? Where de plank road?" and one of whom, crying "Let go me! Let go me!" in response to Henry's clutch and question, "Why—" struck him a knee-buckling blow across the head with the butt or barrel of the rifle which, unlike Henry, he had somehow forgotten to drop in his flight from fury. But this is only the first and most obvious of the ironies that, as Garnett saw, serve to "check the emotional intensity" of the novel and sometimes even reverse, from underneath, the meaning of what is said on the surface.

A case in point is "He was a man," referred to earlier. The sentence or phrase occurs five times in the course of the novel. First: "He suddenly lost concern for himself, and forgot to look at a menacing fate. He became not a man but a member." Next: "He had performed his mistakes in the dark, so he was still a man." The third concerns the whole regiment, badly winded on the march: "Since much of their strength and their breath had vanished, they returned to caution. They were become men again." Another follows their stalwart repulse of a rebel charge. "They gazed about them with looks of uplifted pride, feeling new trust in the grim, always confident weapons in their hands. And they were men." The fifth, on the next-to-last page of the book, applies to Henry alone: "He had been to touch the great death, and found that, after all, it was but the great death. He was a man." The first describes an automatonic melding, while the second reveals an undetected coward. The third portrays humanity recovered through exhaustion. Only the fourth and fifth imply outright manliness in the macho sense and, coming as they do on the heels of success, reflect a sort of congratulatory optimism, not entirely based on fact. The one interpretation common to all five is that they define, at best, the act of rejoining the human race; "they returned to caution." Crane's ultimate irony pertains to the confidence Fleming and his fellows feel at having survived the ultimate challenge of manhood. For if this is Chancellorsville—and it is—Gettysburg is only two months up the road in Pennsylvania, a still more horrendous kind of hellish testing for all involved, including Henry Fleming.

Nor is that by any means the limit of Crane's use of irony as a means of undercutting what he seems to say. Nature herself plays a tricky role in the drama, including its controversial two-line final paragraph, added in New Orleans just before he left for Texas: "Over the river a golden ray of sun came through the leaden hosts of rain clouds." Supposedly this is an upbeat ending, but a look back raises doubts. On the march to the Rappahannock crossing, "the sky overhead was of a fairy blue," and when the regiment halts for the night Henry begins to wonder whether he'll "run when the time comes." He does indeed run next day in the heat of combat, but during a lull just before he takes off rearward he observes "the blue, pure sky and the sun gleaming on the trees and fields" and finds it "surprising that Nature had gone on with her golden process in the midst of so much devilment." He runs, then manages to rejoin his outfit in time for the next day's fighting, and comports himself well in breaking up another rebel charge. As he is congratulating himself on his share in the repulse, he no sooner notices, "the sun now bright and gay in the blue, enameled sky" than he also sees his childhood friend Jimmie Rogers, gut shot and soon to die, "thrashing about in the grass, twisting his shuddering body into many strange postures [and] screaming loudly." The action resumes "under a sapphire sky," and reaches a climax in a charge that is broken off by orders to fall back across the river in the rain. The battle is over, and Crane's ahistorical historical novel ends with that ray of gold. Whether its portent is any more valid than all those others, as a symbol of hope or a confirmation of Henry's newfound resolution, is a question each reader can answer for himself. Yes or no; either will serve. You can even take one and then the other; both will do.

Any true work having to do with war is bound by definition to turn out antiwar in its effect, and so of course does this one. Its beauty obtains in its devotion to truth, in its highly original use of materials that were very much at hand but were neglected until Crane took hold of them. Startling in its contrast to the ruck of books engendered by that fractricidal conflict, fact or fiction, *The Red Badge* is itself the "golden ray" that "came through the hosts of leaden rain clouds."

Stephen Crane's post–*Red Badge* career was upbeat-downbeat, upbeat-downbeat, and finally, under the press of circumstances—debt and deadlines and disease—altogether downbeat. He had seen the problem clearly from the onset of that first deluge of praise, defining it as highly personal. "The majestic forces arrayed against man's true success," he declared in a letter to a friend, "[are] not the world—the world is silly, changeable, any of its decisions can be reversed—but man's own colossal impulses more strong than chains, and I perceived that the fight was not going to be with the world but with yourself."

He had by then, the spring of 1896, completed *George's Mother*, which came out in June, followed by a revised version of *Maggie*, bowdlerized into near gentility at Appleton's insistence. *The Third Violet* began its run as a *McClure's* serial in October, and *The Little Regiment*, a collection of recent Civil War stories, was published in early December. By that time Crane had come down from his hills and was in Jacksonville, Florida, seeking passage on a vessel running arms to Cuba in support of the rebels fighting to throw off the colonial yoke of Spain. While he waited— perhaps on the occasion of what was called "a trip down the line"—he met Cora Howorth Stewart, known locally as Cora Taylor. Six years his senior, of ample proportions, twice married and once divorced, proprietress-operator of a first-class house of assignation called the Hotel de Dream, she was variously described as "a sort of *Tannhäuser* Venus among madams" and "a bi-roxide blonde." They had a full month together, and then on the last night of the year he was off, having secured a berth as a crewman on the filibuster steamer *Commodore*, bound for Cuba with a cargo of rifles and ammunition. He had written of war and now he wanted to see one, even if it was only an insurrection.

What he saw instead, and took part in, was a shipwreck. The heavy-laden *Commodore* ran aground next day, after clearing port, and was hauled off by a Coast Guard vessel. Evidently this operation started her seams; for on January 2, down near Daytona, she foundered and sank. Crane and three others, the captain and an oiler and the cook, managed to get clear in a ten-foot dinghy, riding wave after wave that threatened to engulf them all night long and then at daybreak did just that when they tried for a landing in the heavy surf. The oiler died, struck by the careening boat they had been flung from, but the others made it safely ashore. Crane wrote a graphic newspaper account of the misadventure, headed "Stephen Crane's Own Story," then later—after returning to Jacksonville and his honey-haired Cora, and above all after giving "the detail of [the] thing" time "to filter through [his] blood"—the first of his half dozen greatest stories, titled "The Open Boat," which broke ground for a new kind of fiction, particularly American in nature.

As soon as he was rested from his frustrated exertions in search of one war, he set out in search of another, this time in Greece, where the Turks were making trouble. Back in New York by March, he signed on with Hearst's New York *Journal* to cover the Greco-Turkish War, sailing first for England, and in Greece by early May got his first view of a battle from a grandstand seat on a mountainside near Velestino. Though he was never within eyesight of actual hand-to-hand fighting, he heard individual rifle shots clearly enough to describe "the silken, sliding, tender noise of the bullet and the thud of its impact." What seems to have impressed him most, however, in this first, somewhat offstage experience of combat, was its racket:

> The roll of musketry was tremendous. From a distance it was like tearing a cloth; nearer, it sounded like rain on a tin roof and close up it was just long crash after crash. It was a beautiful sound—beautiful as I had never dreamed. It was more impressive than the roar of Niagara and finer than thunder or avalanche—because it had the wonder of human tragedy in it. It was the most beautiful sound of my experience, barring no symphony. The crash of it was ideal.

All the same, the author of *The Red Badge* was prompt to add, "This is one point of view. Another might be taken from the men who died here."

Before the month was out the war was over, and in June he and Cora—who had joined him after also signing up with Hearst as "Imogene Carter," advertised in the *Journal* as "the first and only woman war correspondent"—took up residence in England, where she assumed still another guise as Mrs. Stephen Crane. They rented a house called Ravensbrook at Oxted, Surrey, a few miles southwest of London, and Crane got to work earning the money they would need to live there in the style to which they expected to become accustomed. During the last half of the year he wrote, along with a number of lesser things, his fifth short novel, *The Monster*, and two more of his best stories, "The Bride Comes to Yellow Sky" and "Death and the Child." Through his British publisher, William Heinemann, he met Joseph Conrad, who soon became a close friend. Year later Conrad said that the excitement in England over the publication of Crane's *Red Badge* was one of the greatest pleasures of his literary life, and he would recall with affection the times they spent together, at work on separate books in the same room. Of their first meeting, in the early fall of 1897, he would say, "I saw a young man of medium stature and slender build, with very steady, penetrating blue eyes, the eyes of a being who not only sees visions but can brood over them to some purpose."

Crane began the new year with a six-week stretch of concentration on a single story, "The Blue Hotel," details of which he had been carrying around in his head since the Nebraska trip, just over three years ago—a lengthy "filtering" process, followed by painstaking composition that produced what many critics have called the best short work of his short writing life. This done, he returned to newspaper sketches and began blocking out a romantic war novel, *Active Service*, based in part on his and Cora's recent sojourn in Greece and the little he had seen of combat at long range. By now the Ravensbrook bills were piling up;

he foresaw months of hectic journalism stretching out before him, a stony road. Then in mid-February the *Maine* blew up in Havana harbor and he saw a way not only to get off the journalistic treadmill but also to attend the only full-scale war he was likely ever to see. What was more, he had it in his mind to see this one from the inside, so to speak. In early April, three weeks before the actual U.S. declaration of war against Spain, he borrowed passage money and boarded a transatlantic liner for New York, where he intended to volunteer for service in the Navy.

But the Navy wouldn't have him. After what may have been the first official diagnosis of the pulmonary tuberculosis that would kill him two years later, he flunked the physical. Undeterred, he turned to Joseph Pulitzer's *World*, signed on as a correspondent, and joined others of his kind waiting at Key West for things to start booming, one hundred miles away across the water. The wait was not long, no longer in fact than the "splendid little war" itself. From June 10, when the Marines landed and took the high ground overlooking Guantanamo Bay, until July 6, when he gave in to exhaustion and a burning fever that required his evacuation one week before the surrender of Santiago, Crane was in the thick of things; Las Guásimas, El Caney, San Juan Hill—he was in on all of them, not only as an observer but also as a participant, serving once as a volunteer signalman under fire, and was cited in dispatches for bravery in action. Moreover, he had done his work so well for Pulitzer, all the while, that Richard Harding Davis himself declared that Crane was the best of all the many correspondents on the scene.

After a brief convalescence in the hospital at Old Point Comfort, Virginia, he returned to New York, shifted from Pulitzer back to Hearst, and set out for Puerto Rico, where he thought the next military action was likely to occur. When it didn't—the occupation was bloodless and the armistice was signed before mid-August—he slipped illegally into Havana, disguised as a tobacco salesman, and lay low while sweating out a recurrence of what by now had been identified as malaria. "The only fact in the universe is that my veins burned and boiled," he declared when he got back to New York in November, ending a heavy three-month stretch of writing. *The Open Boat and Other Stories* had come out in May, adding considerably to his reputation while he was on the way to Key West, and he was intent on striking while the iron was hot. In addition to work on *Active Service* he had completed four Cuban war stories intended for a collection he would call *Wounds in the Rain,* and he was also writing poems to add to a new book of "lines" titled *War Is Kind,* scheduled for publication in May of the following year. Whatever else he was after, off on his own in all this concentrated labor, certainly one of them was money. "Hit him hard," he had told his agent back in October, in a note attached to an article for McClure. "Hit him beastly hard. I have got to have at least fifteen hundred dollars this month, sooner the better. For Christ's sake get me some money quick here by cable."

Evidently he was anxious to get back to Cora, though he had not so much as written her a letter—let alone sent her any cash to help deal with those still-mounting bills at Ravensbrook—since he stole into Havana, back in August. But that too was characteristic. "Stevie is like the wind in scripture. He bloweth whither he listeth," his mother had said of him in his boyhood, and he took no pains to deny it. "I go through life unexplained," he once remarked, and later he added, "I cannot help vanishing and disappearing. It is my foremost trait." In any case, Cora had been looking after herself quite capably for years; it was no doubt one of the things that drew him to her. Finally though, five days before Christmas, he wired her that he would soon be with her, and on the last day of 1898 he sailed.

This was the anniversary of his departure from Jacksonville on the disrupted filibuster expedition, and in that year a great deal had happened to him, most of it strenuous in the extreme, including shipwreck and the open boat, the aborted Greco-Turkish War and the failed Navy physical, behavior so frantic and heedless under fire in Cuba that observing friends considered him downright suicidal, utter exhaustion and recurrent malaria, Puerto Rico and the three-

month Havana writing stretch, and the two hard winter months in New York before sailing. Cora no doubt
could see much of this in his face and form, which
were pale and specter thin. It could even be supposed,
from all this, that he had come back to her to die,
though she probably did not let herself believe it and
she certainly did not speak of it to him or anyone else.
Nor did Crane to her, though he later admitted outright to a friend, "The truth is that Cuba Libre just
about liberated me from this base blue world. The
clockwork is juggling badly."

Still, this last year of the century opened on an encouraging note in England. When Crane arrived he
found Edward Garnett's essay in the December *Acad-
emy* still on display in bookstores. He had at last found
someone who could not only see what he was getting at
but could also see how he had gone about it. "The rare
thing about Mr. Crane's art," Garnett wrote in the
piece he would later expand, "is that he keeps closer to
the surface than any living writer, and, like the great
portrait painters, to a great extent makes the surface
betray the depth." Moreover, 1899 was another three-
book year: *War Is Kind* on schedule in May. *Active
Service* in October, and *The Monster and Other Stories*
(including "The Blue Hotel") in December. All the
while, he continued to add material to what would be
Wounds in the Rain, and he began writing stories
based on his boyhood in Port Jervis, which he called
Whilhomville, as if to say it was a once-upon-a-time

place he knew he would never see again. In addition to all this, he agreed to undertake two books he would have to leave to others to complete: *Great Battles of the World*, contracted for reluctantly with Lippincott's and *The O'Ruddy*, an Irish romance he managed to write two thirds of. There would be no let-up until the very end. One day H. G. Wells asked him what he had in progress, and Crane replied that his agent had lined up some magazine pieces for him. "I got to do them, I got to do them," he said dolefully.

Within a month of his arrival they were settled—if you could call it that—in Brede Place, a massive gray stone pile in Sussex, near Hastings, dating back to the fourteenth century, last remodeled in Queen Elizabeth's time and now half in ruins. A legacy of Winston Churchill's mother's sister's husband, who let them have it for next to no rent, the place had neither plumbing nor electricity, no gas for heat or light, and was believed to be haunted by several ghosts. Cora had large-scale hopes for it, however, and had hired an architect to draw up plans for its restoration. There were three dogs, a span of broad-backed carriage horses, a coachman, a butler named Heather, a cook who drank, a gardener, two maids, and any number of guests, some a good deal more welcome than others: Conrad and Garnett, of course, and Wells and Hueffer and Henry James from nearby Rye. "Life's an entre'acte," Crane was fond of saying, and here was played the comic-dreadful last act of his life.

The occasion was a three-day year's end houseparty for close to forty guests. Cora rented beds from the local hospital and placed the men and women, including husbands and wives, in separate dormitories. Crane tried to interest his English friends in poker, by way of diversion, but found to his distress that they would rather chat than concentrate on the game. "In any decent saloon in America you'd be shot for talking like that at poker," he told them, and gave it up. For the most part he was withdrawn, though not unfriendly. On the final night of the party, the next-to-last full night of the century—indeed, of the millennium—he suffered his first massive hemorrhage. Wells, alarmed, bicycled the seven miles to Rye in the dark for a doctor, but there was little the doctor or anyone else could do, including Cora, except nurse him, which she did.

Just the month before, he had defined himself as "a dry twig on the edge of the bonfire," and now the flames were nearer. Soon he was up and about again, calm in manner though somewhat detached and rather dreamy. Yet he could be testy on occasion, especially on the subject of unwanted visitors, who fretted him here as they had done earlier at Ravensbrook, inquisitive and intrusive. "I must have Egyptian blood in me," he once complained. "Mummies rise from the tomb and come to pay calls that last for days." One of them even ventured to speak of his illness in Cora's presence, and Crane wrote him a short note: "Please have the kindness to keep your mouth

shut about my health in front of Mrs. Crane here-
after. . . . It's all up with me but I will not have her
scared. For some funny woman's reason she likes me.
Mind this."

Winter was yielding to spring and Crane returned
to his desk and the hopeless task of matching with
copy the mounting pile of bills and the weekly payroll,
pegging away alternately at *The O'Ruddy* and one or
another of the *Great Battles*. Then on April 1, as he
leaned down to pat one of the dogs, his mouth filled
with blood. This hemorrhage was far worse than the
first, three months ago, and another the next day was
even more devastating. He took to his bed, this time
for good. Cora sent for a specialist from London, a
greatly admired society doctor, who came to Brede,
examined the patient, pronounced his condition not
serious, collected his £50 fee, and left. Arrangements
were already under way to move Crane to a German
sanatorium, said to be altogether the best, at Baden-
weiler in the Black Forest.

Cora as usual made the move in style, on donated
money that as usual soon ran out. Heather the butler
went with them, along with two nurses, a doctor, and
Crane's favorite dog. They spent several days resting
at the fashionable Lord Warden Hotel in Dover, overlooking the Channel they were soon to cross. Conrad
managed to get there in time to wish his friend well,
though he could see that the hope was fragile. "When
I stopped at the door for another look," he later wrote,
"I saw that he had turned his head on the pillow and

was staring wistfully out of the window at the sails of a cutter yacht that glided slowly across the frame, like a dim shadow against the grey sky."

On May 24, with Crane on a litter, they made the Channel crossing, stopped for a day's rest at Basel, and reached Badenweiler on the 27th. By the week's end he was in delirium. "He lives over everything in dreams," Cora wrote in a letter to their Brede landlord, now a patron, "and talks aloud constantly. It is too awful to hear him try to change places in the Open Boat." But this reliving of his fiction was not for long. In the early morning hours of June 5, 1900, he died.

Cora brought his body back to a London mortuary, where his face was on view for a week through a pane of glass let into the coffin lid, and then on to New York and his native state for burial in Evergreen Cemetery at Hillside, New Jersey. She tried for a time to use what she had learned from him to make her way as a writer, but having little talent or luck for that, she returned to Jacksonville and resumed her traffic in what Shake-speare's Pandarus termed "the hold-door trade." She had sold the Hotel de Dream to join Crane in Greece, and now she acquired another such house, with a less fancy but more dignified name, The Court.

Henry James, when he got the word from Baden-weiler, wrote Wells of "poor Crane's so precipitated and, somehow, so unnecessary extinction," but Willa Cather, remembering how, in Nebraska five years be-fore, his eyes "seemed to be burning themselves out," felt no such shock. She recalled that once, while writing a letter, he asked how to spell some word, explaining, "I haven't time to learn to spell." Her wonder was that he hadn't passed on sooner. "Now that he is dead," she later wrote, "it occurs to me that all his life was a preparation for sudden departure."

Crane himself had found that departure easy, or so he said. Near the end, just before he sailed from Dover, gasping for breath as he spoke, he told a friend at his bedside, "When you come to the hedge . . . that we must all go over . . . it isn't bad. You feel sleepy . . . and you don't care. Just a little dreamy anxiety—which world you're really in. . . . That's all."

Early on, he had defined himself as to what he wanted to be and do, and he did it in words all writers, all readers of Crane, can take to heart: "I understand that a man is born into the world with his own pair of eyes, and he is not at all responsible for his vision—he is merely responsible for his quality of personal honesty. To keep close to this honesty is my supreme ambition. There is sublime egotism in talking of honesty. I, however, do not say that I am honest. I merely say that I am as nearly honest as a weak mental machinery will allow. This aim in life struck me as being the only thing worth while. A man is sure to fail at it, but there is something in the failure."

Note

My sources in this brief study are numerous, but the following three were the main ones:

R. W. Stallman, *Stephen Crane: A Biography*, George Braziller, 1968.

Edwin H. Cady, *Stephen Crane*, Twain Publishers, 1980.

James B. Colvert, *Stephen Crane*, Harcourt Brace Jovanovich, 1984.

Stephen Crane, Prose and Poetry, edited by J. C. Levenson for the Library of America, 1984, has an excellent text for the main body of Crane's work

—S.F.

THE
RED BADGE OF
COURAGE

THE cold passed reluctantly from the earth, and the retiring fogs revealed an army stretched out on the hills, resting. As the landscape changed from brown to green, the army awakened, and began to tremble with eagerness at the noise of rumors. It cast its eyes upon the roads, which were growing from long troughs of liquid mud to proper thoroughfares. A river, amber-tinted in the shadow of its banks, purled at the army's feet; and at night, when the stream had become of a sorrowful blackness, one could see across it the red, eyelike gleam of hostile camp fires set in the low brows of distant hills.

Once a certain tall soldier developed virtues and went resolutely to wash a shirt. He came flying back from a brook waving his garment bannerlike. He was swelled with a tale he had heard from a reliable friend, who had heard it from a

3

truthful cavalryman, who had heard it from his
trustworthy brother, one of the orderlies at division headquarters. He adopted the important air
of a herald in red and gold.

"We're goin' t' move t'morrah—sure," he said
pompously to a group in the company street.
"We're goin' 'way up the river, cut across, an'
come around in behint 'em."

To his attentive audience he drew a loud and
elaborate plan of a very brilliant campaign. When
he had finished, the blue-clothed men scattered
into small arguing groups between the rows of
squat brown huts. A negro teamster who had
been dancing upon a cracker box with the hilari-
ous encouragement of two-score soldiers was
deserted. He sat mournfully down. Smoke drifted
lazily from a multitude of quaint chimneys.

"It's a lie! that's all it is—a thunderin' lie!"
said another private loudly. His smooth face was
flushed, and his hands were thrust sulkily into his
trousers' pockets. He took the matter as an
affront to him. "I don't believe the derned old
army's ever going to move. We're set. I've got
ready to move eight times in the last two weeks,
and we ain't moved yet."

The tall soldier felt called upon to defend the

truth of a rumor he himself had introduced. He and the loud one came near to fighting over it.

A corporal began to swear before the assemblage. He had just put a costly board floor in his house, he said. During the early spring he had refrained from adding extensively to the comfort of his environment because he had felt that the army might start on the march at any moment. Of late, however, he had been impressed that they were in a sort of eternal camp.

Many of the men engaged in a spirited debate. One outlined in a peculiarly lucid manner all the plans of the commanding general. He was opposed by men who advocated that there were other plans of campaign. They clamored at each other, numbers making futile bids for the popular attention. Meanwhile, the soldier who had fetched the rumor bustled about with much importance. He was continually assailed by questions.

"What's up, Jim?"

"Th' army's goin' t' move."

"Ah, what yeh talkin' about? How yeh know it is?"

"Well, yeh kin b'lieve me er not, jest as yeh like. I don't care a hang."

There was much food for thought in the manner in which he replied. He came near to convincing them by disdaining to produce proofs. They grew much excited over it.

There was a youthful private who listened with eager ears to the words of the tall soldier and to the varied comments of his comrades. After receiving a fill of discussions concerning marches and attacks, he went to his hut and crawled through an intricate hole that served it as a door. He wished to be alone with some new thoughts that had lately come to him.

He lay down on a wide bunk that stretched across the end of the room. In the other end, cracker boxes were made to serve as furniture. They were grouped about the fireplace. A picture from an illustrated weekly was upon the log walls, and three rifles were paralleled on pegs. Equipments hung on handy projections, and some tin dishes lay upon a small pile of firewood. A folded tent was serving as a roof. The sunlight, without, beating upon it, made it glow a light yellow shade. A small window shot an oblique square of whiter light upon the cluttered floor. The smoke from the fire at times neglected the clay chimney and wreathed into the room, and

this flimsy chimney of clay and sticks made endless threats to set ablaze the whole establishment.

The youth was in a little trance of astonishment. So they were at last going to fight. On the
morrow, perhaps, there would be a battle, and he
would be in it. For a time he was obliged to labor
to make himself believe. He could not accept
with assurance an omen that he was about to
mingle in one of those great affairs of the earth.

He had, of course, dreamed of battles all his
life—of vague and bloody conflicts that had
thrilled him with their sweep and fire. In visions
he had seen himself in many struggles. He had
imagined peoples secure in the shadow of his
eagle-eyed prowess. But awake he had regarded
battles as crimson blotches on the pages of the
past. He had put them as things of the bygone
with his thought-images of heavy crowns and
high castles. There was a portion of the world's
history which he had regarded as the time of
wars, but it, he thought, had been long gone over
the horizon and had disappeared forever.

From his home his youthful eyes had looked
upon the war in his own country with distrust.
It must be some sort of play affair. He had long
despaired of witnessing a Greeklike struggle.

Such would be no more, he had said. Men were better, or more timid. Secular and religious education had effaced the throat-grappling instinct, or else firm finance held in check the passions.

He had burned several times to enlist. Tales of great movements shook the land. They might not be distinctly Homeric, but there seemed to be much glory in them. He had read of marches, sieges, conflicts, and he had longed to see it all. His busy mind had drawn for him large pictures extravagant in color, lurid with breathless deeds.

But his mother had discouraged him. She had affected to look with some contempt upon the quality of his war ardor and patriotism. She could calmly seat herself and with no apparent difficulty give him many hundreds of reasons why he was of vastly more importance on the farm than on the field of battle. She had had certain ways of expression that told him that her statements on the subject came from a deep conviction. Moreover, on her side, was his belief that her ethical motive in the argument was impregnable.

At last, however, he had made firm rebellion against this yellow light thrown upon the color of his ambitions. The newspapers, the gossip of the village, his own picturings, had aroused him to an uncheckable degree. They were in truth fighting finely down there. Almost every day the newspapers printed accounts of a decisive victory.

One night, as he lay in bed, the winds had carried to him the clangoring of the church bell as some enthusiast jerked the rope frantically to tell the twisted news of a great battle. This voice of the people rejoicing in the night had made him shiver in a prolonged ecstasy of excitement. Later, he had gone down to his mother's room and had spoken thus: "Ma, I'm going to enlist."

"Henry, don't you be a fool," his mother had replied. She had then covered her face with the quilt. There was an end to the matter for that night.

Nevertheless, the next morning he had gone to a town that was near his mother's farm and had enlisted in a company that was forming there. When he had returned home his mother was milking the brindle cow. Four others stood waiting. "Ma, I've enlisted," he had said to her diffidently. There was a short silence. "The Lord's will be done, Henry," she had finally replied, and had then continued to milk the brindle cow.

When he had stood in the doorway with his

soldier's clothes on his back, and with the light of excitement and expectancy in his eyes almost defeating the glow of regret for the home bonds, he had seen two tears leaving their trails on his mother's scarred cheeks.

Still, she had disappointed him by saying nothing whatever about returning with his shield or on it. He had privately primed himself for a beautiful scene. He had prepared certain sentences which he thought could be used with touching effect. But her words destroyed his plans. She had doggedly peeled potatoes and addressed him as follows: "You watch out, Henry, an' take good care of yerself in this here fighting business—you watch out, an' take good care of yerself. Don't go a-thinkin' you can lick the hull rebel army at the start, because yeh can't. Yer jest one little feller amongst a hull lot of others, and yeh've got to keep quiet an' do what they tell yeh. I know how you are, Henry.

"I've knet yeh eight pairs of socks, Henry, and I've put in all yer best shirts, because I want my boy to be jest as warm and comf'able as anybody in the army. Whenever they get holes in 'em, I want yeh to send 'em right-away back to me, so's I kin dern 'em.

"An' allus be careful an' choose yer comp'ny. There's lots of bad men in the army, Henry. The army makes 'em wild, and they like nothing better than the job of leading off a young feller like you, as ain't never been away from home much and has allus had a mother, an' a-learning 'em to drink and swear. Keep clear of them folks, Henry. I don't want yeh to ever do anything, Henry, that yeh would be 'shamed to let me know about. Jest think as if I was a-watchin' yeh. If yeh keep that in yer mind allus, I guess yeh'll come out about right.

"Yeh must allus remember yer father, too, child, an' remember he never drunk a drop of licker in his life, and seldom swore a cross oath.

"I don't know what else to tell yeh, Henry, excepting that yeh must never do no shirking, child, on my account. If so be a time comes when yeh have to be kilt or do a mean thing, why, Henry, don't think of anything 'cept what's right, because there's many a woman has to bear up 'ginst sech things these times, and the Lord 'll take keer of us all.

"Don't forgit about the socks and the shirts, child; and I've put a cup of blackberry jam with yer bundle, because I know yeh like it above all things. Good-by, Henry. Watch out, and be a good boy."

He had, of course, been impatient under the ordeal of this speech. It had not been quite what he expected, and he had borne it with an air of irritation. He departed feeling vague relief.

Still, when he had looked back from the gate, he had seen his mother kneeling among the potato parings. Her brown face, upraised, was stained with tears, and her spare form was quivering. He bowed his head and went on, feeling suddenly ashamed of his purposes.

From his home he had gone to the seminary to bid adieu to many schoolmates. They had thronged about him with wonder and admiration. He had felt the gulf now between them and had swelled with calm pride. He and some of his fellows who had donned blue were quite overwhelmed with privileges for all of one afternoon, and it had been a very delicious thing. They had strutted.

A certain light-haired girl had made vivacious fun at his martial spirit, but there was another and darker girl whom he had gazed at steadfastly, and he thought she grew demure and sad at sight of his blue and brass. As he had walked down the path between the rows of oaks, he had turned his head and detected her at a window watching his departure. As he perceived her, she had immediately begun to stare up through the high tree branches at the sky. He had seen a good deal of flurry and haste in her movement as she changed her attitude. He often thought of it.

On the way to Washington his spirit had soared. The regiment was fed and caressed at station after station until the youth had believed that he must be a hero. There was a lavish expenditure of bread and cold meats, coffee, and pickles and cheese. As he basked in the smiles of the girls and was patted and complimented by the old men, he had felt growing within him the strength to do mighty deeds of arms.

After complicated journeying with many pauses, there had come months of monotonous life in a camp. He had had the belief that real war was a series of death struggles with small time in between for sleep and meals; but since his regiment had come to the field the army had done little but sit still and try to keep warm.

He was brought then gradually back to his old ideas. Greeklike struggles would be no more. Men were better, or more timid. Secular and religious education had effaced the throat-grappling instinct, or else firm finance held in check the passions.

He had grown to regard himself merely as a part of a vast blue demonstration. His province was to look out, as far as he could, for his personal comfort. For recreation he could twiddle his thumbs and speculate on the thoughts which must agitate the minds of the generals. Also, he was drilled and drilled and reviewed, and drilled and drilled and reviewed.

The only foes he had seen were some pickets along the river bank. They were a sun-tanned, philosophical lot, who sometimes shot reflectively at the blue pickets. When reproached for this afterward, they usually expressed sorrow, and swore by their gods that the guns had exploded without their permission. The youth, on guard duty one night, conversed across the stream with one of them. He was a slightly ragged man, who spat skillfully between his shoes and possessed a great fund of bland and infantile assurance. The youth liked him personally.

"Yank," the other had informed him, "yer a right dum good feller." This sentiment, floating to him upon the still air, had made him temporarily regret war.

Various veterans had told him tales. Some talked of gray, bewhiskered hordes who were advancing with relentless curses and chewing tobacco with unspeakable valor; tremendous bodies of fierce soldiery who were sweeping along like the Huns. Others spoke of tattered and eternally hungry men who fired despondent powders. "They'll charge through hell's fire an' brimstone t' git a holt on a haversack, an' sech stomachs ain't a-lastin' long," he was told. From the stories, the youth imagined the red, live bones sticking out through slits in the faded uniforms.

Still, he could not put a whole faith in veterans' tales, for recruits were their prey. They talked much of smoke, fire, and blood, but he could not tell how much might be lies. They persistently yelled, "Fresh fish!" at him, and were in no wise to be trusted.

However, he perceived now that it did not greatly matter what kind of soldiers he was going to fight, so long as they fought, which fact no one disputed. There was a more serious problem. He lay in his bunk pondering upon it. He tried to mathematically prove to himself that he would not run from a battle.

Previously he had never felt obliged to wrestle too seriously with this question. In his life he had taken certain things for granted, never challenging his belief in ultimate success, and bothering little about means and roads. But here he was confronted with a thing of moment. It had suddenly appeared to him that perhaps in a battle he might run. He was forced to admit that as far as war was concerned he knew nothing of himself.

A sufficient time before he would have allowed the problem to kick its heels at the outer portals of his mind, but now he felt compelled to give serious attention to it.

A little panic-fear grew in his mind. As his imagination went forward to a fight, he saw hideous possibilities. He contemplated the lurking menaces of the future, and failed in an effort to see himself standing stoutly in the midst of them. He recalled his visions of broken-bladed glory, but in the shadow of the impending tumult he suspected them to be impossible pictures.

He sprang from the bunk and began to pace nervously to and fro. "Good Lord, what's th' matter with me?" he said aloud.

He felt that in this crisis his laws of life were useless. Whatever he had learned of himself was here of no avail. He was an unknown quantity. He saw that he would again be obliged to experiment as he had in early youth. He must accumulate information of himself, and meanwhile he resolved to remain close upon his guard lest those qualities of which he knew nothing should everlastingly disgrace him. "Good Lord!" he repeated in dismay.

After a time the tall soldier slid dexterously through the hole. The loud private followed. They were wrangling.

"That's all right," said the tall soldier as he entered. He waved his hand expressively. "You can believe me or not, jest as you like. All you got to do is to sit down and wait as quiet as you can. Then pretty soon you'll find out I was right."

His comrade grunted stubbornly. For a moment he seemed to be searching for a formidable reply. Finally he said: "Well, you don't know everything in the world, do you?"

"Didn't say I knew everything in the world," retorted the other sharply. He began to stow various articles snugly into his knapsack.

The youth, pausing in his nervous walk, looked down at the busy figure. "Going to be a battle, sure, is there, Jim?" he asked.

"Of course there is," replied the tall soldier. "Of course there is. You jest wait 'til tomorrow, and you'll see one of the biggest battles ever was. You jest wait."

"Thunder!" said the youth.

"Oh, you'll see fighting this time, my boy, what'll be regular out-and-out fighting," added the tall soldier, with the air of a man who is about to exhibit a battle for the benefit of his friends.

"Huh!" said the loud one from a corner.

"Well," remarked the youth, "like as not this story'll turn out jest like them others did."

"Not much it won't," replied the tall soldier, exasperated. "Not much it won't. Didn't the cavalry all start this morning?" He glared about him. No one denied his statement. "The cavalry started this morning," he continued. "They say there ain't hardly any cavalry left in camp. They're going to Richmond, or some place, while we fight all the Johnnies. It's some dodge like that. The regiment's got orders, too. A feller what seen 'em go to headquarters told me a little while ago. And they're raising blazes all over camp—anybody can see that."

"Shucks!" said the loud one.

The youth remained silent for a time. At last he spoke to the tall soldier. "Jim!"

"What?"

"How do you think the reg'ment 'll do?"

"Oh, they'll fight all right, I guess, after they once get into it," said the other with cold judgment. He made a fine use of the third person. "There's been heaps of fun poked at 'em because they're new of course, and all that; but they'll fight all right, I guess."

"Think any of the boys 'll run?" persisted the youth.

"Oh, there may be a few of 'em run, but there's them kind in every regiment, 'specially when they first goes under fire," said the other in a tolerant way. "Of course it might happen that the hull kit-and-boodle might start and run, if some big fighting came first-off, and then again they might stay and fight like fun. But you can't bet on nothing. Of course they ain't never been under fire yet, and it ain't likely they'll lick the hull rebel army all-to-oncet the firs' time; but I think they'll fight better than some, if worse than others. That's the way I figger. They call the reg'ment 'Fresh fish' and everything; but the boys come of good stock, and most of 'em 'll fight like sin after they oncet git shootin'," he added, with a mighty emphasis on the last four words.

"Oh, you think you know—" began the loud soldier with scorn.

The other turned savagely upon him. They had a rapid altercation, in which they fastened upon each other various strange epithets.

The youth at last interrupted them. "Did you ever think you might run yourself, Jim?" he asked. On concluding the sentence he laughed as if he had meant to aim a joke. The loud soldier also giggled.

The tall private waved his hand. "Well," said he profoundly, "I've thought it might get too hot for Jim Conklin in some of them scrimmages, and if a whole lot of boys started and run, why, I s'pose I'd start and run. And if I once started to run, I'd run like the devil, and no mistake. But if everybody was a-standing and a-fighting, why,

I'd stand and fight. Be jiminey, I would. I'll bet on it."

"Huh!" said the loud one.

The youth of this tale felt gratitude for these words of his comrade. He had feared that all of the untried men possessed a great and correct confidence. He now was in a measure reassured.

CHAPTER II

THE next morning the youth discovered that his tall comrade had been the fast-flying messenger of a mistake. There was much scoffing at the latter by those who had yesterday been firm adherents of his views, and there was even a little sneering by men who had never believed the rumor. The tall one fought with a man from Chatfield Corners and beat him severely.

The youth felt, however, that his problem was in no wise lifted from him. There was, on the contrary, an irritating prolongation. The tale had created in him a great concern for himself. Now, with the newborn question in his mind, he was compelled to sink back into his old place as part of a blue demonstration.

For days he made ceaseless calculations, but they were all wondrously unsatisfactory. He found that he could establish nothing. He finally concluded that the only way to prove himself was to go into the blaze, and then figuratively to watch his legs to discover their merits and faults. He reluctantly admitted that he could not sit still and with a mental slate and pencil derive an answer. To gain it, he must have blaze, blood, and danger, even as a chemist requires this, that, and the other. So he fretted for an opportunity.

Meanwhile he continually tried to measure himself by his comrades. The tall soldier, for one, gave him some assurance. This man's serene unconcern dealt him a measure of confidence, for he had known him since childhood, and from his intimate knowledge he did not see how he could be capable of anything that was beyond him, the youth. Still, he thought that his comrade might be mistaken about himself. Or, on the other hand, he might be a man heretofore doomed to peace and obscurity, but, in reality, made to shine in war.

The youth would have liked to have discovered another who suspected himself. A sympathetic comparison of mental notes would have been a joy to him.

He occasionally tried to fathom a comrade with seductive sentences. He looked about to find men in the proper mood. All attempts failed to bring forth any statement which looked in any way like a confession to those doubts which he privately acknowledged in himself. He was afraid to make an open declaration of his concern, because he dreaded to place some unscrupulous confidant upon the high plane of the unconfessed from which elevation he could be derided.

In regard to his companions his mind wavered between two opinions, according to his mood. Sometimes he inclined to believing them all heroes. In fact, he usually admitted in secret the superior development of the higher qualities in others. He could conceive of men going very insignificantly about the world bearing a load of courage unseen, and, although he had known many of his comrades through boyhood, he began to fear that his judgment of them had been blind. Then, in other moments, he flouted these theories, and assured himself that his fellows were all privately wondering and quaking.

His emotions made him feel strange in the presence of men who talked excitedly of a prospective battle as of a drama they were about to witness, with nothing but eagerness and curiosity apparent in their faces. It was often that he suspected them to be liars.

He did not pass such thoughts without severe condemnation of himself. He dinned reproaches at times. He was convicted by himself of many shameful crimes against the gods of traditions.

In his great anxiety his heart was continually clamoring at what he considered the intolerable slowness of the generals. They seemed content to perch tranquilly on the river bank, and leave him bowed down by the weight of a great problem. He wanted it settled forthwith. He could not long bear such a load, he said. Sometimes his anger at the commanders reached an acute stage, and he grumbled about the camp like a veteran.

One morning, however, he found himself in the ranks of his prepared regiment. The men were whispering speculations and recounting the old rumors. In the gloom before the break of the day their uniforms glowed a deep purple hue. From across the river the red eyes were still peering. In the eastern sky there was a yellow patch like a rug laid for the feet of the coming sun; and against it, black and patternlike, loomed the gigantic figure of the colonel on a gigantic horse.

From off in the darkness came the trampling of feet. The youth could occasionally see dark shadows that moved like monsters. The regiment stood at rest for what seemed a long time. The youth grew impatient. It was unendurable the way these affairs were managed. He wondered how long they were to be kept waiting.

As he looked all about him and pondered upon the mystic gloom, he began to believe that at any moment the ominous distance might be aflare, and the rolling crashes of an engagement come to his ears. Staring once at the red eyes across the river, he conceived them to be growing larger, as the orbs of a row of dragons advancing. He turned toward the colonel and saw him lift his gigantic arm and calmly stroke his mustache.

At last he heard from along the road at the foot of the hill the clatter of a horse's galloping hoofs. It must be the coming of orders. He bent forward, scarce breathing. The exciting clickety-click, as it grew louder and louder, seemed to be beating upon his soul. Presently a horesman with jangling equipment drew rein before the colonel of the regiment. The two held a short, sharp-worded conversation. The men in the foremost ranks craned their necks.

As the horseman wheeled his animal and galloped away he turned to shout over his shoulder, "Don't forget that box of cigars!" The colonel mumbled in reply. The youth wondered what a box of cigars had to do with war.

A moment later the regiment went swinging off into the darkness. It was now like one of those moving monsters wending with many feet. The air was heavy, and cold with dew. A mass of wet grass, marched upon, rustled like silk.

There was an occasional flash and glimmer of steel from the backs of all these huge crawling reptiles. From the road came creakings and grumblings as some surly guns were dragged away.

The men stumbled along still muttering speculations. There was a subdued debate. Once a man fell down, and as he reached for his rifle a comrade, unseeing, trod upon his hand. He of the injured fingers swore bitterly and aloud. A low tittering laugh went among his fellows.

Presently they passed into a roadway and marched forward with easy strides. A dark regiment moved before them, and from behind also came the tinkle of equipments on the bodies of marching men.

The rushing yellow of the developing day went on behind their backs. When the sunrays at last struck full and mellowingly upon the earth, the youth saw that the landscape was streaked with two long, thin, black columns which disappeared on the brow of a hill in front and rearward vanished in a wood. They were like two serpents crawling from the cavern of the night.

The river was not in view. The tall soldier burst into praises of what he thought to be his powers of perception.

Some of the tall one's companions cried with emphasis that they, too, had evolved the same thing, and they congratulated themselves upon it. But there were others who said that the tall one's plan was not the true one at all. They persisted with other theories. There was a vigorous discussion.

The youth took no part in them. As he walked along in careless line he was engaged with his own eternal debate. He could not hinder himself from dwelling upon it. He was despondent and sullen, and threw shifting glances about him. He looked ahead, often expecting to hear from the advance the rattle of firing.

But the long serpents crawled slowly from hill to hill without bluster of smoke. A dun-colored cloud of dust floated away to the right. The sky overhead was of a fairy blue.

The youth studied the faces of his companions,

ever on the watch to detect kindred emotions. He suffered disappointment. Some ardor of the air which was causing the veteran commands to move with glee—almost with song—had infected the new regiment. The men began to speak of victory as of a thing they knew. Also, the tall soldier received his vindication. They were certainly going to come around in behind the enemy. They expressed commiseration for that part of the army which had been left upon the river bank, felicitating themselves upon being a part of a blasting host.

The youth, considering himself as separated from the others, was saddened by the blithe and merry speeches that went from rank to rank. The company wags all made their best endeavors. The regiment tramped to the tune of laughter.

The blatant soldier often convulsed whole files by his biting sarcasms aimed at the tall one.

And it was not long before all the men seemed to forget their mission. Whole brigades grinned in unison, and regiments laughed.

A rather fat soldier attempted to pilfer a horse from a dooryard. He planned to load his knapsack upon it. He was escaping with his prize when a young girl rushed from the house and grabbed the animal's mane. There followed a wrangle. The young girl, with pink cheeks and shining eyes, stood like a dauntless statue.

The observant regiment, standing at rest in the roadway, whooped at once, and entered whole-souled upon the side of the maiden. The men became so engrossed in this affair that they entirely ceased to remember their own large war. They jeered the piratical private, and called attention to various defects in his personal appearance; and they were wildly enthusiastic in support of the young girl.

To her, from some distance, came bold advice. "Hit him with a stick."

There were crows and catcalls showered upon him when he retreated without the horse. The regiment rejoiced at his downfall. Loud and vociferous congratulations were showered upon the maiden, who stood panting and regarding the troops with defiance.

At nightfall the column broke into regimental pieces, and the fragments went into the fields to camp. Tents sprang up like strange plants. Camp fires, like red, peculiar blossoms, dotted the night.

The youth kept from intercourse with his companions as much as circumstances would allow him. In the evening he wandered a few paces into the gloom. From this little distance the many fires, with the black forms of men passing to and fro before the crimson rays, made weird and satanic effects.

He lay down in the grass. The blades pressed tenderly against his cheek. The moon had been lighted and was hung in a treetop. The liquid stillness of the night enveloping him made him feel vast pity for himself. There was a caress in the soft winds; and the whole mood of the darkness, he thought, was one of sympathy for himself in his distress.

He wished, without reserve, that he was at home again making the endless rounds from the house to the barn, from the barn to the fields, from the fields to the barn, from the barn to the house. He remembered he had often cursed the brindle cow and her mates, and had sometimes flung milking stools. But, from his present point of view, there was a halo of happiness about each of their heads, and he would have sacrificed all the brass buttons on the continent to have been enabled to return to them. He told himself that he was not formed for a soldier. And he mused seriously upon the radical differences between himself and those men who were dodging implike around the fires.

As he mused thus he heard the rustle of grass, and, upon turning his head, discovered the loud soldier. He called out, "Oh, Wilson!"

The latter approached and looked down. "Why, hello, Henry, is it you? What you doing here?"

"Oh, thinking," said the youth.

The other sat down and carefully lighted his pipe. "You're getting blue, my boy. You're looking thundering peeked. What the dickens is wrong with you?"

"Oh, nothing," said the youth.

The loud soldier launched then into the subject of the anticipated fight. "Oh, we've got 'em now!" As he spoke his boyish face was wreathed in a gleeful smile, and his voice had an exultant ring. "We've got 'em now. At last, by the eternal thunders, we'll lick 'em good!

"If the truth was known," he added, more soberly, "*they've* licked *us* about every clip up to now; but this time—this time—we'll lick 'em good!"

"I thought you was objecting to this march a little while ago," said the youth coldly.

"Oh, it wasn't that," explained the other. "I don't mind marching, if there's going to be fighting at the end of it. What I hate is this getting moved here and moved there, with no good coming of it, as far as I can see, excepting sore feet and damned short rations."

"Well, Jim Conklin says we'll get a plenty of fighting this time."

"He's right for once, I guess, though I can't see how it come. This time we're in for a big battle, and we've got the best end of it, certain sure. Gee rod! how we will thump 'em!"

He arose and began to pace to and fro excitedly. The thrill of his enthusiasm made him walk with an elastic step. He was sprightly, vigorous, fiery in his belief in success. He looked into the future with clear, proud eye, and he swore with the air of an old soldier.

The youth watched him for a moment in silence. When he finally spoke his voice was as bitter as dregs. "Oh, you're going to do great things, I s'pose!"

The loud soldier blew a thoughtful cloud of smoke from his pipe. "Oh, I don't know," he remarked with dignity; "I don't know. I s'pose I'll do as well as the rest. I'm going to try like thunder." He evidently complimented himself upon the modesty of this statement.

"How do you know you won't run when the time comes?" asked the youth.

"Run?" said the loud one; "run?—of course not!" He laughed.

"Well," continued the youth, "lots of good-a-'nough men have thought they was going to do great things before the fight, but when the time come they skedaddled."

"Oh, that's all true, I s'pose," replied the other; "but I'm not going to skedaddle. The man that bets on my running will lose his money, that's all." He nodded confidently.

"Oh, shucks!" said the youth. "You ain't the bravest man in the world, are you?"

"No, I ain't," exclaimed the loud soldier indignantly; "and I didn't say I was the bravest man in the world, neither. I said I was going to do my share of fighting—that's what I said. And I am, too. Who are you, anyhow? You talk as if you thought you was Napoleon Bonaparte." He glared at the youth for a moment, and then strode away.

The youth called in a savage voice after his comrade: "Well, you needn't git mad about it!"

But the other continued on his way and made no reply.

He felt alone in space when his injured comrade had disappeared. His failure to discover any mite of resemblance in their viewpoints made him more miserable than before. No one seemed to be wrestling with such a terrific personal problem. He was a mental outcast.

He went slowly to his tent and stretched himself on a blanket by the side of the snoring tall soldier. In the darkness he saw visions of a thousand-tongued fear that would babble at his back and cause him to flee, while others were going coolly about their country's business. He admitted that he would not be able to cope with this monster. He felt that every nerve in his body would be an ear to hear the voices, while other men would remain stolid and deaf.

And as he sweated with the pain of these thoughts, he could hear low, serene sentences. "I'll bid five." "Make it six." "Seven." "Seven goes."

He stared at the red, shivering reflection of a fire on the white wall of his tent until, exhausted and ill from the monotony of his suffering, he fell asleep.

CHAPTER III

WHEN another night came the columns, changed to purple streaks, filed across two pontoon bridges. A glaring fire wine-tinted the waters of the river. Its rays, shining upon the moving masses of troops, brought forth here and there sudden gleams of silver or gold. Upon the other shore a dark and mysterious range of hills was curved against the sky. The insect voices of the night sang solemnly.

After this crossing the youth assured himself that at any moment they might be suddenly and fearfully assaulted from the caves of the lowering woods. He kept his eyes watchfully upon the darkness.

But his regiment went unmolested to a camping place, and its soldiers slept the brave sleep of wearied men. In the morning they were routed out with early energy, and hustled along a narrow road that led deep into the forest.

It was during this rapid march that the regiment lost many of the marks of a new command.

The men had begun to count the miles upon their fingers, and they grew tired. "Sore feet an' damned short rations, that's all," said the loud soldier. There were perspiration and grumblings. After a time they began to shed their knapsacks. Some tossed them unconcernedly down; others hid them carefully, asserting their plans to return for them at some convenient time. Men extricated themselves from thick shirts. Presently few carried anything but their necessary clothing, blankets, haversacks, canteens, and arms and ammunition. "You can now eat and shoot," said the tall soldier to the youth. "That's all you want to do."

There was sudden change from the ponderous infantry of theory to the light and speedy infantry of practice. The regiment, relieved of a burden, received a new impetus. But there was much loss of valuable knapsacks, and, on the whole, very good shirts.

But the regiment was not yet veteranlike in

appearance. Veteran regiments in the army were likely to be very small aggregations of men. Once, when the command had first come to the field, some perambulating veterans, noting the length of their column, had accosted them thus: "Hey, fellers, what brigade is that?" And when the men had replied that they formed a regiment and not a brigade, the older soldiers had laughed, and said, "O Gawd!"

Also, there was too great a similarity in the hats. The hats of a regiment should properly represent the history of headgear for a period of years. And, moreover, there were no letters of faded gold speaking from the colors. They were new and beautiful, and the color bearer habitually oiled the pole.

Presently the army again sat down to think. The odor of the peaceful pines was in the men's nostrils. The sound of monotonous axe blows rang through the forest, and the insects, nodding upon their perches, crooned like old women. The youth returned to his theory of a blue demonstration.

One gray dawn, however, he was kicked in the leg by the tall soldier, and then, before he was entirely awake, he found himself running down a wood road in the midst of men who were panting from the first effects of speed. His canteen banged rhythmically upon his thigh, and his haversack bobbed softly. His musket bounced a trifle from his shoulder at each stride and made his cap feel uncertain upon his head.

He could hear the men whisper jerky sentences: "Say—what's all this—about?" "What th' thunder—we—skedaddlin' this way fer?" "Billie—keep off m' feet. Yeh run—like a cow." And the loud soldier's shrill voice could be heard: "What th' devil they in sich a hurry for?"

The youth thought the damp fog of early morning moved from the rush of a great body of troops. From the distance came a sudden spatter of firing.

He was bewildered. As he ran with his comrades he strenuously tried to think, but all he knew was that if he fell down those coming behind would tread upon him. All his faculties seemed to be needed to guide him over and past obstructions. He felt carried along by a mob.

The sun spread disclosing rays, and, one by one, regiments burst into view like armed men just born of the earth. The youth perceived that the time had come. He was about to be measured. For a moment he felt in the face of his great trial like a babe, and the flesh over his heart seemed very thin. He seized time to look about him calculatingly.

But he instantly saw that it would be impossible for him to escape from the regiment. It inclosed him. And there were iron laws of tradition and law on four sides. He was in a moving box.

As he perceived this fact it occurred to him that he had never wished to come to the war. He had not enlisted of his free will. He had been dragged by the merciless government. And now they were taking him out to be slaughtered.

The regiment slid down a bank and wallowed across a little stream. The mournful current moved slowly on, and from the water, shaded black, some white bubble eyes looked at the men.

As they climbed the hill on the farther side artillery began to boom. Here the youth forgot many things as he felt a sudden impulse of curiosity. He scrambled up the bank with a speed that could not be exceeded by a blood-thirsty man.

He expected a battle scene.

There were some little fields girted and squeezed by a forest. Spread over the grass and in among the tree trunks, he could see knots and waving lines of skirmishers who were running hither and thither and firing at the landscape. A dark battle line lay upon a sun-struck clearing that gleamed orange color. A flag fluttered.

Other regiments floundered up the bank. The brigade was formed in line of battle, and after a pause started slowly through the woods in the rear of the receding skirmishers, who were continually melting into the scene to appear again farther on. They were always busy as bees, deeply absorbed in their little combats.

The youth tried to observe everything. He did not use care to avoid trees and branches, and his forgotten feet were constantly knocking against stones or getting entangled in briers. He was aware that these battalions with their commotions were woven red and startling into the gentle fabric of softened greens and browns. It looked to be a wrong place for a battle field.

The skirmishers in advance fascinated him. Their shots into thickets and at distant and prominent trees spoke to him of tragedies—hidden, mysterious, solemn.

Once the line encountered the body of a dead soldier. He lay upon his back staring at the sky. He was dressed in an awkward suit of yellowish brown. The youth could see that the soles of his shoes had been worn to the thinness of writing paper, and from a great rent in one the dead foot projected piteously. And it was as if fate had betrayed the soldier. In death it exposed to his enemies that poverty which in life he had perhaps concealed from his friends.

The ranks opened covertly to avoid the corpse. The invulnerable dead man forced a way for himself. The youth looked keenly at the ashen face. The wind raised the tawny beard. It moved as if a hand were stroking it. He vaguely desired to walk around and around the body and stare; the impulse of the living to try to read in dead eyes the answer to the Question.

During the march the ardor which the youth had acquired when out of view of the field rapidly faded to nothing. His curiosity was quite easily satisfied. If an intense scene had caught him with its wild swing as he came to the top of the bank, he might have gone roaring on. This advance upon Nature was too calm. He had opportunity to reflect. He had time in which to wonder about himself and to attempt to probe his sensations.

Absurd ideas took hold upon him. He thought that he did not relish the landscape. It threatened him. A coldness swept over his back, and it is true that his trousers felt to him that they were no fit for his legs at all.

A house standing placidly in distant fields had to him an ominous look. The shadows of the woods were formidable. He was certain that in this vista there lurked fierce-eyed hosts. The swift thought came to him that the generals did not know what they were about. It was all a trap. Suddenly those close forests would bristle with rifle barrels. Ironlike brigades would appear in the rear. They were all going to be sacrificed. The generals were stupids. The enemy would presently swallow the whole command. He glared about him, expecting to see the stealthy approach of his death.

He thought that he must break from the ranks and harangue his comrades. They must not all be killed like pigs, and he was sure it would come to pass unless they were informed of these dangers. The generals were idiots to send them marching into a regular pen. There was but one pair of eyes in the corps. He would step forth and make a speech. Shrill and passionate words came to his lips.

The line, broken into moving fragments by the ground, went calmly on through fields and woods. The youth looked at the men nearest him, and saw, for the most part, expressions of deep interest, as if they were investigating something that had fascinated them. One or two stepped with overvaliant airs as if they were already plunged into war. Others walked as upon thin ice. The greater part of the untested men appeared quiet and absorbed. They were going to look at war, the red animal—war, the blood-swollen god. And they were deeply engrossed in this march.

As he looked the youth gripped his outcry at his throat. He saw that even if the men were tottering with fear they would laugh at his warning. They would jeer him, and, if practicable, pelt him with missiles. Admitting that he might be wrong, a frenzied declamation of the kind would turn him into a worm.

He assumed, then, the demeanor of one who knows that he is doomed alone to unwritten responsibilities. He lagged, with tragic glances at the sky.

He was surprised presently by the young lieutenant of his company, who began heartily to
beat him with a sword, calling out in a loud and
insolent voice: "Come, young man, get up into
ranks there. No skulking'll do here." He mended
his pace with suitable haste. And he hated the
lieutenant, who had no appreciation of fine
minds. He was a mere brute.

After a time the brigade was halted in the
cathedral light of a forest. The busy skirmishers
were still popping. Through the aisles of the
wood could be seen the floating smoke from their
rifles. Sometimes it went up in little balls, white
and compact.

During this halt many men in the regiment
began erecting tiny hills in front of them. They
used stones, sticks, earth, and anything they
thought might turn a bullet. Some built comparatively large ones, while others seemed content
with little ones.

This procedure caused a discussion among the
men. Some wished to fight like duelists, believing
it to be correct to stand erect and be, from their
feet to their foreheads, a mark. They said they
scorned the devices of the cautious. But the others scoffed in reply, and pointed to the veterans

on the flanks who were digging at the ground like terriers. In a short time there was quite a barricade along the regimental fronts. Directly, however, they were ordered to withdraw from that place.

This astounded the youth. He forgot his stewing over the advance movement. "Well, then, what did they march us out here for?" he demanded of the tall soldier. The latter with calm faith began a heavy explanation, although he had been compelled to leave a little protection of stones and dirt to which he had devoted much care and skill.

When the regiment was aligned in another position each man's regard for his safety caused another line of small intrenchments. They ate their noon meal behind a third one. They were moved from this one also. They were marched from place to place with apparent aimlessness.

The youth had been taught that a man became another thing in a battle. He saw his salvation in such a change. Hence this waiting was an ordeal to him. He was in a fever of impatience. He considered that there was denoted a lack of purpose on the part of the generals. He began to complain to the tall soldier. "I can't stand this much longer," he cried. "I don't see what good it does to make us wear out our legs for nothin'." He wished to return to camp, knowing that this affair was a blue demonstration; or else to go into a battle and discover that he had been a fool in his doubts, and was, in truth, a man of traditional courage. The strain of present circumstances he felt to be intolerable.

The philosophical tall soldier measured a sandwich of cracker and pork and swallowed it in a nonchalant manner. "Oh, I suppose we must go reconnoitering around the country jest to keep 'em from getting too close, or to develop 'em, or something."

"Huh!" said the loud soldier.

"Well," cried the youth, still fidgeting, "I'd rather do anything 'most than go tramping 'round the country all day doing no good to nobody and jest tiring ourselves out."

"So would I," said the loud soldier. "It ain't right. I tell you if anybody with any sense was a-runnin' this army it—"

"Oh, shut up!" roared the tall private. "You little fool. You little damn' cuss. You ain't had that there coat and them pants on for six months, and yet you talk as if—"

"Well, I wanta do some fighting anyway," interrupted the other. "I didn't come here to walk. I could 'ave walked to home—'round an 'round the barn, if I jest wanted to walk."

The tall one, red-faced, swallowed another sandwich as if taking poison in despair.

But gradually, as he chewed, his face became again quiet and contented. He could not range in fierce argument in the presence of such sandwiches. During his meals he always wore an air of blissful contemplation of the food he had swallowed. His spirit seemed then to be communing with the viands.

He accepted new environment and circumstance with great coolness, eating from his haversack at every opportunity. On the march he went along with the stride of a hunter, objecting to neither gait nor distance. And he had not raised his voice when he had been ordered away from three little protective piles of earth and stone, each of which had been an engineering feat worthy of being made sacred to the name of his grandmother.

In the afternoon the regiment went out over the same ground it had taken in the morning. The landscape then ceased to threaten the youth. He had been close to it and become familiar with it.

When, however, they began to pass into a new region, his old fears of stupidity and incompetence reassailed him, but this time he doggedly let them babble. He was occupied with his problem, and in his desperation he concluded that the stupidity did not greatly matter.

Once he thought he had concluded that it would be better to get killed directly and end his troubles. Regarding death thus out of the corner of his eye, he conceived it to be nothing but rest, and he was filled with a momentary astonishment that he should have made an extraordinary commotion over the mere matter of getting killed. He would die; he would go to some place where he would be understood. It was useless to expect appreciation of his profound and fine senses from such men as the lieutenant. He must look to the grave for comprehension.

The skirmish fire increased to a long clattering sound. With it was mingled far-away cheering. A battery spoke.

Directly the youth could see the skirmishers running. They were pursued by the sound of musketry fire. After a time the hot, dangerous flashes of the rifles were visible. Smoke clouds went slowly and insolently across the fields like observant phantoms. The din became crescendo, like the roar of an oncoming train.

A brigade ahead of them and on the right went into action with a rending roar. It was as if it had exploded. And thereafter it lay stretched in the distance behind a long gray wall, that one was obliged to look twice at to make sure that it was smoke.

The youth, forgetting his neat plan of getting killed, gazed spellbound. His eyes grew wide and busy with the action of the scene. His mouth was a little ways open.

Of a sudden he felt a heavy and sad hand laid upon his shoulder. Awakening from his trance of observation he turned and beheld the loud soldier.

"It's my first and last battle, old boy," said the latter, with intense gloom. He was quite pale and his girlish lip was trembling.

"Eh?" murmured the youth in great astonishment.

"It's my first and last battle, old boy," continued the loud soldier. "Something tells me—"

"What?"

"I'm a gone coon this first time and—and I w-want you to take these here things—to—my—folks." He ended in a quavering sob of pity for himself. He handed the youth a little packet done up in a yellow envelope.

"Why, what the devil—" began the youth again.

But the other gave him a glance as from the depths of a tomb, and raised his limp hand in a prophetic manner and turned away.

CHAPTER IV

THE brigade was halted in the fringe of a grove. The men crouched among the trees and pointed their restless guns out at the fields. They tried to look beyond the smoke.

Out of this haze they could see running men. Some shouted information and gestured as they hurried.

The men of the new regiment watched and listened eagerly, while their tongues ran on in gossip of the battle. They mouthed rumors that had flown like birds out of the unknown.

"They say Perry has been driven in with big loss."

"Yes, Carrott went t' th' hospital. He said he was sick. That smart lieutenant is commanding 'G' Company. Th' boys say they won't be under Carrott no more if they all have t' desert. They allus knew he was a—"

"Hannises' batt'ry is took."

"It ain't either. I saw Hannises' batt'ry off on th' left not more'n fifteen minutes ago."

"Well—"

"Th' general, he ses he is goin' t' take th' hull command of th' 304th when we go inteh action, an' then he ses we'll do sech fightin' as never another one reg'ment done."

"They say we're catchin' it over on th' left. They say th' enemy driv' our line inteh a devil of a swamp an' took Hannises' batt'ry."

"No sech thing. Hannises' batt'ry was 'long here 'bout a minute ago."

"That young Hasbrouck, he makes a good off'cer. He ain't afraid 'a nothin'."

"I met one of th' 148th Maine boys an' he ses his brigade fit th' hull rebel army fer four hours over on th' turnpike road an' killed about five thousand of 'em. He ses one more sech fight as that an' th' war 'll be over."

"Bill wasn't scared either. No, sir! It wasn't that. Bill ain't a-gittin' scared easy. He was jest mad, that's what he was. When that feller trod on his hand, he up an' sed that he was willin' t' give his hand t' his country, but he be dumbed if he was goin' t' have every dumb bushwacker in th' kentry walkin' 'round on it. So he went t' th' hospital disregardless of th' fight. Three fingers was crunched. Th' dern doctor wanted t' amputate 'm, an' Bill, he raised a heluva row, I hear. He's a funny feller."

The din in front swelled to a tremendous chorus. The youth and his fellows were frozen to silence. They could see a flag that tossed in the smoke angrily. Near it were the blurred and agitated forms of troops. There came a turbulent stream of men across the fields. A battery changing position at a frantic gallop scattered the stragglers right and left.

A shell screaming like a storm banshee went over the huddled heads of the reserves. It landed in the grove, and exploding redly flung the brown earth. There was a little shower of pine needles.

Bullets began to whistle among the branches and nip at the trees. Twigs and leaves came sailing down. It was as if a thousand axes, wee and invisible, were being wielded. Many of the men were constantly dodging and ducking their heads.

The lieutenant of the youth's company was shot in the hand. He began to swear so wondrously that a nervous laugh went along the regimental line. The officer's profanity sounded conventional. It relieved the tightened senses of the new men. It was as if he had hit his fingers with a tack hammer at home.

He held the wounded member carefully away from his side so that the blood would not drip upon his trousers.

The captain of the company, tucking his sword under his arm, produced a handkerchief and began to bind with it the lieutenant's wound. And they disputed as to how the binding should be done.

The battle flag in the distance jerked about madly. It seemed to be struggling to free itself from an agony. The billowing smoke was filled with horizontal flashes.

Men running swiftly emerged from it. They grew in numbers until it was seen that the whole command was fleeing. The flag suddenly sank down as if dying. Its motion as it fell was a gesture of despair.

Wild yells came from behind the walls of smoke. A sketch in gray and red dissolved into a moblike body of men who galloped like wild horses.

The veteran regiments on the right and left of

the 304th immediately began to jeer. With the passionate song of the bullets and the banshee shrieks of shells were mingled loud catcalls and bits of facetious advice concerning places of safety.

But the new regiment was breathless with horror. "Gawd! Saunders's got crushed!" whispered the man at the youth's elbow. They shrank back and crouched as if compelled to await a flood.

The youth shot a swift glance along the blue ranks of the regiment. The profiles were motionless, carven; and afterward he remembered that the color sergeant was standing with his legs apart, as if he expected to be pushed to the ground.

The following throng went whirling around the flank. Here and there were officers carried along on the stream like exasperated chips. They were striking about them with their swords and with their left fists, punching every head they could reach. They cursed like highwaymen.

A mounted officer displayed the furious anger of a spoiled child. He raged with his head, his arms, and his legs.

Another, the commander of the brigade, was galloping about bawling. His hat was gone and his clothes were awry. He resembled a man who had come from bed to go to a fire. The hoofs of his horse often threatened the heads of the running men, but they scampered with singular fortune. In this rush they were apparently all deaf and blind. They heeded not the largest and longest of the oaths that were thrown at them from all directions.

Frequently over this tumult could be heard the grim jokes of the critical veterans; but the retreating men apparently were not even conscious of the presence of an audience.

The battle reflection that shone for an instant in the faces on the mad current made the youth feel that forceful hands from heaven would not have been able to have held him in place if he could have got intelligent control of his legs.

There was an appalling imprint upon these faces. The struggle in the smoke had pictured an exaggeration of itself on the bleached cheeks and in the eyes wild with one desire.

The sight of this stampede exerted a floodlike force that seemed able to drag sticks and stones and men from the ground. They of the reserves had to hold on. They grew pale and firm, and red and quaking.

The youth achieved one little thought in the midst of this chaos. The composite monster which had caused the other troops to flee had not then appeared. He resolved to get a view of it, and then, he thought he might very likely run better than the best of them.

CHAPTER V

THERE were moments of waiting. The youth thought of the village street at home before the arrival of the circus parade on a day in the spring. He remembered how he had stood, a small, thrillful boy, prepared to follow the dingy lady upon the white horse, or the band in its faded chariot. He saw the yellow road, the lines of expectant people, and the sober houses. He particularly remembered an old fellow who used to sit upon a cracker box in front of the store and feign to despise such exhibitions. A thousand details of color and form surged in his mind. The old fellow upon the cracker box appeared in middle prominence.

Some one cried, "Here they come!"

There was rustling and muttering among the men. They displayed a feverish desire to have every possible cartridge ready to their hands. The boxes were pulled around into various positions, and adjusted with great care. It was as if seven hundred new bonnets were being tried on.

The tall soldier, having prepared his rifle, produced a red handkerchief of some kind. He was engaged in knotting it about his throat with exquisite attention to its position, when the cry was repeated up and down the line in a muffled roar of sound.

"Here they come! Here they come!" Gun locks clicked.

Across the smoke-infested fields came a brown swarm of running men who were giving shrill yells. They came on, stooping and swinging their rifles at all angles. A flag, tilted forward, sped near the front.

As he caught sight of them the youth was momentarily startled by a thought that perhaps his gun was not loaded. He stood trying to rally his faltering intellect so that he might recollect the moment when he had loaded, but he could not.

A hatless general pulled his dripping horse to a stand near the colonel of the 304th. He shook his fist in the other's face. "You've got to hold 'em back!" he shouted, savagely; "you've got to hold 'em back!"

In his agitation the colonel began to stammer. "A-all r-right, General, all right, by Gawd! We-we'll do our—we-we'll d-d-do—do our best, General." The general made a passionate gesture and galloped away. The colonel, perchance to relieve his feelings, began to scold like a wet parrot. The youth, turning swiftly to make sure that the rear was unmolested, saw the commander regarding his men in a highly resentful manner, as if he regretted above everything his association with them.

The man at the youth's elbow was mumbling, as if to himself: "Oh, we're in for it now! oh, we're in for it now!"

The captain of the company had been pacing excitedly to and fro in the rear. He coaxed in schoolmistress fashion, as to a congregation of boys with primers. His talk was an endless repetition. "Reserve your fire, boys—wait till they get close up—don't be damned fools . . ."

Perspiration streamed down the youth's face, which was soiled like that of a weeping urchin. He frequently, with a nervous movement, wiped his eyes with his coat sleeve. His mouth was still a little way open.

He got the one glance at the foe-swarming

field in front of him, and instantly ceased to debate the question of his piece being loaded. Before he was ready to begin—before he had announced to himself that he was about to fight—he threw the obedient, well-balanced rifle into position and fired a first wild shot. Directly he was working at his weapon like an automatic affair.

He suddenly lost concern for himself, and forgot to look at a menacing fate. He became not a man but a member. He felt that something of which he was a part—a regiment, an army, a cause, or a country—was in a crisis. He was welded into a common personality which was dominated by a single desire. For some moments he could not flee, no more than a little finger can commit a revolution from a hand.

If he had thought the regiment was about to be annihilated perhaps he could have amputated himself from it. But its noise gave him assurance. The regiment was like a firework that, once ignited, proceeds superior to circumstances until its blazing vitality fades. It wheezed and banged with a mighty power. He pictured the ground before it as strewn with the discomfited.

There was a consciousness always of the pres-

ence of his comrades about him. He felt the subtle battle brotherhood more potent even than the
cause for which they were fighting. It was a mysterious fraternity born of the smoke and danger
of death.

He was at a task. He was like a carpenter who
has made many boxes, making still another box,
only there was furious haste in his movements.
He, in his thoughts, was careering off in other
places, even as the carpenter who as he works
whistles and thinks of his friend or his enemy, his
home or a saloon. And these jolted dreams were
never perfect to him afterward, but remained a
mass of blurred shapes.

Presently he began to feel the effects of the war
atmosphere—a blistering sweat, a sensation that
his eyeballs were about to crack like hot stones. A
burning roar filled his ears.

Following this came a red rage. He developed
the acute exasperation of a pestered animal, a
well-meaning cow worried by dogs. He had a
mad feeling against his rifle, which could only be
used against one life at a time. He wished to rush
forward and strangle with his fingers. He craved
a power that would enable him to make a world-
sweeping gesture and brush all back. His impo-

tency appeared to him, and made his rage into that of a driven beast.

Buried in the smoke of many rifles his anger was directed not so much against the men who he knew were rushing toward him as against the swirling battle phantoms which were choking him, stuffing their smoke robes down his parched throat. He fought frantically for respite for his senses, for air, as a babe being smothered attacks the deadly blankets.

There was a blare of heated rage mingled with a certain expression of intentness on all faces. Many of the men were making low-toned noises with their mouths, and these subdued cheers, snarls, imprecations, prayers, made a wild, bar-baric song that went as an undercurrent of sound, strange and chantlike with the resounding chords of the war march. The man at the youth's elbow was babbling. In it there was something soft and tender like the monologue of a babe. The tall soldier was swearing in a loud voice. From his lips came a black procession of curious oaths. Of a sudden another broke out in a queru-lous way like a man who has mislaid his hat. "Well, why don't they send supports? Do they think—"

The youth in his battle sleep heard this as one who dozes hears.

There was a singular absence of heroic poses. The men bending and surging in their haste and rage were in every impossible attitude. The steel ramrods clanked and clanged with incessant din as the men pounded them furiously into the hot rifle barrels. The flaps of the cartridge boxes were all unfastened, and bobbed idiotically with each movement. The rifles, once loaded, were jerked to the shoulder and fired without apparent aim into the smoke or at one of the blurred and shifting forms which, upon the field before the regiment, had been growing larger and larger like puppets under a magician's hand.

The officers, at their intervals, rearward, neglected to stand in picturesque attitudes. They were bobbing to and fro roaring directions and encouragements. The dimensions of their howls were extraordinary. They expended their lungs with prodigal wills. And often they nearly stood upon their heads in their anxiety to observe the enemy on the other side of the tumbling smoke.

The lieutenant of the youth's company had encountered a soldier who had fled screaming at the first volley of his comrades. Behind the lines these two were acting a little isolated scene. The man was blubbering and staring with sheeplike eyes at the lieutenant, who had seized him by the collar and was pommeling him. He drove him back into the ranks with many blows. The soldier went mechanically, dully, with his animal-like eyes upon the officer. Perhaps there was to him a divinity expressed in the voice of the other—stern, hard, with no reflection of fear in it. He tried to reload his gun, but his shaking hands prevented. The lieutenant was obliged to assist him.

The men dropped here and there like bundles. The captain of the youth's company had been killed in an early part of the action. His body lay stretched out in the position of a tired man resting, but upon his face there was an astonished and sorrowful look, as if he thought some friend had done him an ill turn. The babbling man was grazed by a shot that made the blood stream widely down his face. He clapped both hands to his head. "Oh!" he said, and ran. Another grunted suddenly as if he had been struck by a club in the stomach. He sat down and gazed ruefully. In his eyes there was mute, indefinite reproach. Farther up the line a man, standing behind a tree, had had his knee joint splintered by a ball. Immediately he had dropped his rifle and gripped the tree with both arms. And there he remained, clinging desperately and crying for assistance that he might withdraw his hold upon the tree.

At last an exultant yell went along the quivering line. The firing dwindled from an uproar to a last vindictive popping. As the smoke slowly eddied away, the youth saw that the charge had been repulsed. The enemy were scattered into reluctant groups. He saw a man climb to the top of the fence, straddle the rail, and fire a parting shot. The waves had receded, leaving bits of dark *débris* upon the ground.

Some in the regiment began to whoop frenziedly. Many were silent. Apparently they were trying to contemplate themselves.

After the fever had left his veins, the youth thought that at last he was going to suffocate. He became aware of the foul atmosphere in which he had been struggling. He was grimy and dripping like a laborer in a foundry. He grasped his canteen and took a long swallow of the warmed water.

A sentence with variations went up and down

the line. "Well, we've helt 'em back. We've helt 'em back; derned if we haven't." The men said it blissfully, leering at each other with dirty smiles.

The youth turned to look behind him and off to the right and off to the left. He experienced the joy of a man who at last finds leisure in which to look about him.

Under foot there were a few ghastly forms motionless. They lay twisted in fantastic contortions. Arms were bent and heads were turned in incredible ways. It seemed that the dead men must have fallen from some great height to get into such positions. They looked to be dumped out upon the ground from the sky.

From a position in the rear of the grove a battery was throwing shells over it. The flash of the guns startled the youth at first. He thought they were aimed directly at him. Through the trees he watched the black figures of the gunners as they worked swiftly and intently. Their labor seemed a complicated thing. He wondered how they could remember its formula in the midst of confusion.

The guns squatted in a row like savage chiefs. They argued with abrupt violence. It was a grim pow-wow. Their busy servants ran hither and thither.

A small procession of wounded men were going drearily toward the rear. It was a flow of blood from the torn body of the brigade.

To the right and to the left were the dark lines of other troops. Far in front he thought he could see lighter masses protruding in points from the forest. They were suggestive of unnumbered thousands.

Once he saw a tiny battery go dashing along the line of the horizon. The tiny riders were beating the tiny horses.

From a sloping hill came the sound of cheerings and clashes. Smoke welled slowly through the leaves.

Batteries were speaking with thunderous oratorical effort. Here and there were flags, the red in the stripes dominating. They splashed bits of warm color upon the dark lines of troops.

The youth felt the old thrill at the sight of the emblems. They were like beautiful birds strangely undaunted in a storm.

As he listened to the din from the hillside, to a deep pulsating thunder that came from afar to the left, and to the lesser clamors which came from many directions, it occurred to him that they were fighting, too, over there, and over there, and over there. Heretofore he had supposed that all the battle was directly under his nose.

As he gazed around him the youth felt a flash of astonishment at the blue, pure sky and the sun gleaming on the trees and fields. It was surprising that Nature had gone tranquilly on with her golden process in the midst of so much devilment.

CHAPTER VI

THE youth awakened slowly. He came gradually back to a position from which he
could regard himself. For moments he had been
scrutinizing his person in a dazed way as if he
had never before seen himself. Then he picked
up his cap from the ground. He wriggled in his
jacket to make a more comfortable fit, and kneeling relaced his shoe. He thoughtfully mopped his
reeking features.

So it was all over at last! The supreme trial had
been passed. The red, formidable difficulties of
war had been vanquished.

He went into an ecstasy of self-satisfaction. He
had the most delightful sensations of his life.
Standing as if apart from himself, he viewed that
last scene. He perceived that the man who had
fought thus was magnificent.

He felt that he was a fine fellow. He saw himself even with those ideals which he had considered as far beyond him. He smiled in deep gratification.

Upon his fellows he beamed tenderness and good will. "Gee! ain't it hot, hey?" he said affably to a man who was polishing his steaming face with his coat sleeves.

"You bet!" said the other, grinning sociably. "I never seen sech dumb hotness." He sprawled out luxuriously on the ground. "Gee, yes! An' I hope we don't have no more fightin' till a week from Monday."

There were some handshakings and deep speeches with men whose features were familiar, but with whom the youth now felt the bonds of tied hearts. He helped a cursing comrade to bind up a wound of the shin.

But, of a sudden, cries of amazement broke out along the ranks of the new regiment. "Here they come ag'in! Here they come ag'in!" The man who had sprawled upon the ground started up and said, "Gosh!"

The youth turned quick eyes upon the field. He discerned forms begin to swell in masses out of a distant wood. He again saw the tilted flag speeding forward.

The shells, which had ceased to trouble the regiment for a time, came swirling again, and exploded in the grass or among the leaves of the trees. They looked to be strange war flowers bursting into fierce bloom.

The men groaned. The luster faded from their eyes. Their smudged countenances now expressed a profound dejection. They moved their stiffened bodies slowly, and watched in sullen mood the frantic approach of the enemy. The slaves toiling in the temple of this god began to feel rebellion at his harsh tasks.

They fretted and complained each to each. "Oh, say, this is too much of a good thing! Why can't somebody send up supports?"

"We ain't never goin' to stand this second banging. I didn't come here to fight the hull damn' rebel army."

There was one who raised a doleful cry. "I wish Bill Smithers had trod on my hand, insteader me treddin' on his'n." The sore joints of the regiment creaked as it painfully floundered into position to repulse.

The youth stared. Surely, he thought, this impossible thing was not about to happen. He waited as if he expected the enemy to suddenly stop, apologize, and retire bowing. It was all a mistake.

But the firing began somewhere on the regimental line and ripped along in both directions. The level sheets of flame developed great clouds of smoke that tumbled and tossed in the mild wind near the ground for a moment, and then rolled through the ranks as through a grate. The clouds were tinged an earthlike yellow in the sunrays and in the shadow were a sorry blue. The flag was sometimes eaten and lost in this mass of vapor, but more often it projected, sun-touched, resplendent.

Into the youth's eyes there came a look that one can see in the orbs of a jaded horse. His neck was quivering with nervous weakness and the muscles of his arms felt numb and bloodless. His hands, too, seemed large and awkward as if he was wearing invisible mittens. And there was a great uncertainty about his knee joints.

The words that comrades had uttered previous to the firing began to recur to him. "Oh, say, this is too much of a good thing! What do they take us for—why don't they send supports? I didn't come here to fight the hull damned rebel army."

He began to exaggerate the endurance, the

skill, and the valor of those who were coming. Himself reeling from exhaustion, he was astonished beyond measure at such persistency. They must be machines of steel. It was very gloomy struggling against such affairs, wound up perhaps to fight until sundown.

He slowly lifted his rifle and catching a glimpse of the thickspread field he blazed at a cantering cluster. He stopped then and began to peer as best he could through the smoke. He caught changing views of the ground covered with men who were all running like pursued imps, and yelling.

To the youth it was an onslaught of redoubtable dragons. He became like the man who lost his legs at the approach of the red and green monster. He waited in a sort of a horrified, listening attitude. He seemed to shut his eyes and wait to be gobbled.

A man near him who up to this time had been working feverishly at his rifle suddenly stopped and ran with howls. A lad whose face had borne an expression of exalted courage, the majesty of he who dares give his life, was, at an instant, smitten abject. He blanched like one who has come to the edge of a cliff at midnight and is suddenly made aware. There was a revelation. He, too, threw down his gun and fled. There was no shame in his face. He ran like a rabbit.

Others began to scamper away through the smoke. The youth turned his head, shaken from his trance by this movement as if the regiment was leaving him behind. He saw the few fleeting forms.

He yelled then with fright and swung about. For a moment, in the great clamor, he was like a proverbial chicken. He lost the direction of safety. Destruction threatened him from all points.

Directly he began to speed toward the rear in great leaps. His rifle and cap were gone. His unbuttoned coat bulged in the wind. The flap of his cartridge box bobbed wildly, and his canteen, by its slender cord, swung out behind. On his face was the horror of those things which he imagined.

The lieutenant sprang forward bawling. The youth saw his features wrathfully red, and saw him make a dab with his sword. His one thought of the incident was that the lieutenant was a peculiar creature to feel interested in such matters upon this occasion.

He ran like a blind man. Two or three times he fell down. Once he knocked his shoulder so heavily against a tree that he went headlong.

Since he had turned his back upon the fight his fears had been wondrously magnified. Death about to thrust him between the shoulder blades was far more dreadful than death about to smite him between the eyes. When he thought of it later, he conceived the impression that it is better to view the appalling than to be merely within hearing. The noises of the battle were like stones; he believed himself liable to be crushed.

As he ran on he mingled with others. He dimly saw men on his right and on his left, and he heard footsteps behind him. He thought that all the regiment was fleeing, pursued by these ominous crashes.

In his flight the sound of these following footsteps gave him his one meager relief. He felt vaguely that death must make a first choice of the men who were nearest; the initial morsels for the dragons would be then those who were following him. So he displayed the zeal of an insane sprinter in his purpose to keep them in the rear. There was a race.

As he, leading, went across a little field, he

found himself in a region of shells. They hurtled over his head with long wild screams. As he listened he imagined them to have rows of cruel teeth that grinned at him. Once one lit before him and the livid lightning of the explosion effectually barred the way in his chosen direction. He groveled on the ground and then springing up went careering off through some bushes.

He experienced a thrill of amazement when he came within view of a battery in action. The men there seemed to be in conventional moods, altogether unaware of the impending annihilation. The battery was disputing with a distant antagonist and the gunners were wrapped in admiration of their shooting. They were continually bending in coaxing postures over the guns. They seemed to be patting them on the back and encouraging them with words. The guns, stolid and undaunted, spoke with dogged valor.

The precise gunners were coolly enthusiastic. They lifted their eyes every chance to the smoke-wreathed hillock from whence the hostile battery addressed them. The youth pitied them as he ran. Methodical idiots! Machine-like fools! The refined joy of planting shells in the midst of the other battery's formation would appear a little thing when the infantry came swooping out of the woods.

The face of a youthful rider, who was jerking his frantic horse with an abandon of temper he might display in a placid barnyard, was impressed deeply upon his mind. He knew that he looked upon a man who would presently be dead.

Too, he felt a pity for the guns, standing, six good comrades, in a bold row.

He saw a brigade going to the relief of its pestered fellows. He scrambled upon a wee hill and watched it sweeping finely, keeping formation in difficult places. The blue of the line was crusted with steel color, and the brilliant flags projected. Officers were shouting.

This sight also filled him with wonder. The brigade was hurrying briskly to be gulped into the infernal mouths of the war god. What manner of men were they, anyhow? Ah, it was some wondrous breed! Or else they didn't comprehend—the fools.

A furious order caused commotion in the artillery. An officer on a bounding horse made maniacal motions with his arms. The teams went swinging up from the rear, the guns were whirled about, and the battery scampered away. The cannon with their noses poked slantingly at the ground grunted and grumbled like stout men, brave but with objections to hurry.

The youth went on, moderating his pace since he had left the place of noises.

Later he came upon a general of division seated upon a horse that pricked its ears in an interested way at the battle. There was a great gleaming of yellow and patent leather about the saddle and bridle. The quiet man astride looked mouse-colored upon such a splendid charger.

A jingling staff was galloping hither and thither. Sometimes the general was surrounded by horsemen and at other times he was quite alone. He looked to be much harassed. He had the appearance of a business man whose market is swinging up and down.

The youth went slinking around this spot. He went as near as he dared trying to overhear words. Perhaps the general, unable to comprehend chaos, might call upon him for information. And he could tell him. He knew all concerning it. Of a surety the force was in a fix, and any fool could see that if they did not retreat while they had opportunity—why—

He felt that he would like to thrash the general, or at least approach and tell him in plain words exactly what he thought him to be. It was criminal to stay calmly in one spot and make no effort to stay destruction. He loitered in a fever of eagerness for the division commander to apply to him.

As he warily moved about, he heard the general call out irritably: "Tompkins, go over an' see Taylor, an' tell him not t' be in such an all-fired hurry; tell him t' halt his brigade in th' edge of th' woods; tell him t' detach a reg'ment—say I think th' center 'll break if we don't help it out some; tell him t' hurry up."

A slim youth on a fine chestnut horse caught these swift words from the mouth of his superior. He made his horse bound into a gallop almost from a walk in his haste to go upon his mission. There was a cloud of dust.

A moment later the youth saw the general bounce excitedly in his saddle.

"Yes, by heavens, they have!" The officer leaned forward. His face was aflame with excitement. "Yes, by heavens, they've held 'im! They've held 'im!"

He began to blithely roar at his staff: "We'll wallop 'im now. We'll wallop 'im now. We've got 'em sure." He turned suddenly upon an aide: "Here—you—Jones—quick—ride after Tompkins—see Taylor—tell him t' go in—everlastingly—like blazes—anything."

As another officer sped his horse after the first messenger, the general beamed upon the earth like a sun. In his eyes was a desire to chant a pæan. He kept repeating, "They've held 'em, by heavens!"

His excitement made his horse plunge, and he merrily kicked and swore at it. He held a little carnival of joy on horseback.

CHAPTER VII

THE youth cringed as if discovered in a crime. By heavens, they had won after all! The imbecile line had remained and become victors. He could hear cheering.

He lifted himself upon his toes and looked in the direction of the fight. A yellow fog lay wallowing on the treetops. From beneath it came the clatter of musketry. Hoarse cries told of an advance.

He turned away amazed and angry. He felt that he had been wronged.

He had fled, he told himself, because annihilation approached. He had done a good part in saving himself, who was a little piece of the army. He had considered the time, he said, to be one in which it was the duty of every little piece to rescue itself if possible. Later the officers could fit the little pieces together again, and make a battle front. If none of the little pieces were wise enough to save themselves from the flurry of death at such a time, why, then, where would be the army? It was all plain that he had proceeded according to very correct and commendable rules. His actions had been sagacious things. They had been full of strategy. They were the work of a master's legs.

Thoughts of his comrades came to him. The brittle blue line had withstood the blows and won. He grew bitter over it. It seemed that the blind ignorance and stupidity of those little pieces had betrayed him. He had been overturned and crushed by their lack of sense in holding the position, when intelligent deliberation would have convinced them that it was impossible. He, the enlightened man who looks afar in the dark, had fled because of his superior perceptions and knowledge. He felt a great anger against his comrades. He knew it could be proved that they had been fools.

He wondered what they would remark when later he appeared in camp. His mind heard howls of derision. Their destiny would not enable them to understand his sharper point of view.

He began to pity himself acutely. He was ill

used. He was trodden beneath the feet of an iron injustice. He had proceeded with wisdom and from the most righteous motives under heaven's blue only to be frustrated by hateful circumstances.

A dull, animal-like rebellion against his fellows, war in the abstract, and fate grew within him. He shambled along with bowed head, his brain in a tumult of agony and despair. When he looked loweringly up, quivering at each sound, his eyes had the expression of those of a criminal who thinks his guilt little and his punishment great, and knows that he can find no words.

He went from the fields into a thick wood, as if resolved to bury himself. He wished to get out of hearing of the cracking shots which were to him like voices.

The ground was cluttered with vines and bushes, and the trees grew close and spread out like bouquets. He was obliged to force his way with much noise. The creepers, catching against his legs, cried out harshly as their sprays were torn from the barks of trees. The swishing saplings tried to make known his presence to the world. He could not conciliate the forest. As he made his way, it was always calling out protestations. When he separated embraces of trees and vines the disturbed foliages waved their arms and turned their face leaves toward him. He dreaded lest these noisy motions and cries should bring men to look at him. So he went far, seeking dark and intricate places.

After a time the sound of musketry grew faint and the cannon boomed in the distance. The sun, suddenly apparent, blazed among the trees. The insects were making rhythmical noises. They seemed to be grinding their teeth in unison. A woodpecker stuck his impudent head around the side of a tree. A bird flew on lighthearted wing.

Off was the rumble of death. It seemed now that Nature had no ears.

This landscape gave him assurance. A fair field holding life. It was the religion of peace. It would die if its timid eyes were compelled to see blood. He conceived Nature to be a woman with a deep aversion to tragedy.

He threw a pine cone at a jovial squirrel, and he ran with chattering fear. High in a treetop he stopped, and, poking his head cautiously from behind a branch, looked down with an air of trepidation.

The youth felt triumphant at this exhibition. There was the law, he said. Nature had given him a sign. The squirrel, immediately upon recognizing danger, had taken to his legs without ado. He did not stand stolidly baring his furry belly to the missile, and die with an upward glance at the sympathetic heavens. On the contrary, he had fled as fast as his legs could carry him; and he was but an ordinary squirrel, too— doubtless no philosopher of his race. The youth wended, feeling that Nature was of his mind. She re-enforced his argument with proofs that lived where the sun shone.

Once he found himself almost into a swamp. He was obliged to walk upon bog tufts and watch his feet to keep from the oily mire. Pausing at one time to look about him he saw, out at some black water, a small animal pounce in and emerge directly with a gleaming fish.

The youth went again into the deep thickets. The brushed branches made a noise that drowned the sounds of cannon. He walked on, going from obscurity into promises of a greater obscurity.

At length he reached a place where the high, arching boughs made a chapel. He softly pushed the green doors aside and entered. Pine needles were a gentle brown carpet. There was a religious half light.

Near the threshold he stopped, horror-stricken at the sight of a thing.

He was being looked at by a dead man who was seated with his back against a columnlike tree. The corpse was dressed in a uniform that once had been blue, but was now faded to a melancholy shade of green. The eyes, staring at the youth, had changed to the dull hue to be seen on the side of a dead fish. The mouth was open. Its red had changed to an appalling yellow. Over the gray skin of the face ran little ants. One was trundling some sort of a bundle along the upper lip.

The youth gave a shriek as he confronted the thing. He was for moments turned to stone before it. He remained staring into the liquid-looking eyes. The dead man and living man exchanged a long look. Then the youth cautiously put one hand behind him and brought it against a tree. Leaning upon this he retreated, step by step, with his face still toward the thing. He feared that if he turned his back the body might spring up and stealthily pursue him.

The branches, pushing against him, threatened

to throw him over upon it. His unguided feet, too, caught aggravatingly in brambles; and with it all he received a subtle suggestion to touch the corpse. As he thought of his hand upon it he shuddered profoundly.

At last he burst the bonds which had fastened him to the spot and fled, unheeding the underbrush. He was pursued by a sight of the black ants swarming greedily upon the gray face and venturing horribly near to the eyes.

After a time he paused, and, breathless and panting, listened. He imagined some strange voice would come from the dead throat and squawk after him in horrible menaces.

The trees about the portals of the chapel moved soughingly in a soft wind. A sad silence was upon the little guarding edifice.

CHAPTER VIII

THE trees began softly to sing a hymn of twilight. The sun sank until slanted bronze
rays struck the forest. There was a lull in the
noises of insects as if they had bowed their beaks
and were making a devotional pause. There was
silence save for the chanted chorus of the trees.

Then, upon this stillness, there suddenly broke
a tremendous clangor of sounds. A crimson roar
came from the distance.

The youth stopped. He was transfixed by this
terrific medley of all noises. It was as if worlds
were being rended. There was the ripping sound
of musketry and the breaking crash of artillery.

His mind flew in all directions. He conceived
the two armies to be at each other panther fashion. He listened for a time. Then he began to run
in the direction of the battle. He saw that it was
an ironical thing for him to be running thus

toward that which he had been at such pains to avoid. But he said, in substance, to himself that if the earth and the moon were about to clash, many persons would doubtless plan to get upon the roofs to witness the collision.

As he ran, he became aware that the forest had stopped its music, as if at last becoming capable of hearing the foreign sounds. The trees hushed and stood motionless. Everything seemed to be listening to the crackle and clatter and ear-shaking thunder. The chorus pealed over the still earth.

It suddenly occurred to the youth that the fight in which he had been was, after all, but perfunctory popping. In the hearing of this present din he was doubtful if he had seen real battle scenes. This uproar explained a celestial battle; it was tumbling hordes a-struggle in the air.

Reflecting, he saw a sort of humor in the point of view of himself and his fellows during the late encounter. They had taken themselves and the enemy very seriously and had imagined that they were deciding the war. Individuals must have supposed that they were cutting the letters of their names deep into everlasting tablets of brass, or enshrining their reputations forever in the hearts of their countrymen, while, as to fact, the affair would appear in printed reports under a meek and immaterial title. But he saw that it was good, else, he said, in battle every one would surely run save forlorn hopes and their ilk.

He went rapidly on. He wished to come to the edge of the forest that he might peer out.

As he hastened, there passed through his mind pictures of stupendous conflicts. His accumulated thought upon such subjects was used to form scenes. The noise was as the voice of an eloquent being, describing.

Sometimes the brambles formed chains and tried to hold him back. Trees, confronting him, stretched out their arms and forbade him to pass. After its previous hostility this new resistance of the forest filled him with a fine bitterness. It seemed that Nature could not be quite ready to kill him.

But he obstinately took roundabout ways, and presently he was where he could see long gray walls of vapor where lay battle lines. The voices of cannon shook him. The musketry sounded in long irregular surges that played havoc with his ears. He stood regardant for a moment. His eyes had an awestruck expression. He gawked in the direction of the fight.

Presently he proceeded again on his forward way. The battle was like the grinding of an immense and terrible machine to him. Its complexities and powers, its grim processes, fascinated him. He must go close and see it produce corpses.

He came to a fence and clambered over it. On the far side, the ground was littered with clothes and guns. A newspaper, folded up, lay in the dirt. A dead soldier was stretched with his face hidden in his arm. Farther off there was a group of four or five corpses keeping mournful company. A hot sun had blazed upon the spot.

In this place the youth felt that he was an invader. This forgotten part of the battle ground was owned by the dead men, and he hurried, in the vague apprehension that one of the swollen forms would rise and tell him to begone.

He came finally to a road from which he could see in the distance dark and agitated bodies of troops, smoke-fringed. In the lane was a blood-stained crowd streaming to the rear. The wounded men were cursing, groaning, and wailing. In the air, always, was a mighty swell of sound that it seemed could sway the earth. With the courageous words of the artillery and the spiteful sentences of the musketry mingled red cheers. And from this region of noises came the steady current of the maimed.

One of the wounded men had a shoeful of blood. He hopped like a schoolboy in a game. He was laughing hysterically.

One was swearing that he had been shot in the arm through the commanding general's misman-agement of the army. One was marching with an air imitative of some sublime drum major. Upon his features was an unholy mixture of merriment and agony. As he marched he sang a bit of dog-gerel in an high and quavering voice:

"Sing a song 'a vic'try,
A pocketful 'a bullets,
Five an' twenty dead men
Baked in a—pie."

Parts of the procession limped and staggered to this tune.

Another had the gray seal of death already upon his face. His lips were curled in hard lines and his teeth were clinched. His hands were bloody from where he had pressed them upon his wound. He seemed to be awaiting the moment when he should pitch headlong. He stalked like the specter of a soldier, his eyes burning with the power of a stare into the unknown.

There were some who proceeded sullenly, full of anger at their wounds, and ready to turn upon anything as an obscure cause.

An officer was carried along by two privates. He was peevish. "Don't joggle so, Johnson, yeh fool," he cried. "Think m' leg is made of iron? If yeh can't carry me decent, put me down an' let some one else do it."

He bellowed at the tottering crowd who blocked the quick march of his bearers. "Say, make way there, can't yeh? Make way, dickens take it all."

They sulkily parted and went to the roadsides. As he was carried past they made pert remarks to him. When he raged in reply and threatened them, they told him to be damned.

The shoulder of one of the tramping bearers knocked heavily against the spectral soldier who was staring into the unknown.

The youth joined this crowd and marched along with it. The torn bodies expressed the awful machinery in which the men had been entangled.

Orderlies and couriers occasionally broke through the throng in the roadway, scattering wounded men right and left, galloping on, followed by howls. The melancholy march was continually disturbed by the messengers, and sometimes by bustling batteries that came swinging and thumping down upon them, the officers shouting orders to clear the way.

There was a tattered man, fouled with dust, blood and powder stain from hair to shoes, who trudged quietly at the youth's side. He was listening with eagerness and much humility to the lurid descriptions of a bearded sergeant. His lean features wore an expression of awe and admiration. He was like a listener in a country store to wondrous tales told among the sugar barrels. He eyed the story-teller with unspeakable wonder. His mouth was agape in yokel fashion.

The sergeant, taking note of this, gave pause to his elaborate history while he administered a sardonic comment. "Be keerful, honey, you'll be a-ketchin' flies," he said.

The tattered man shrank back abashed.

After a time he began to sidle near to the youth, and in a diffident way try to make him a friend. His voice was gentle as a girl's voice and his eyes were pleading. The youth saw with surprise that the soldier had two wounds, one in the head, bound with a blood-soaked rag, and the other in the arm, making that member dangle like a broken bough.

After they had walked together for some time the tattered man mustered sufficient courage to speak. "Was pretty good fight, wasn't it?" he timidly said. The youth, deep in thought, glanced up at the bloody and grim figure with its lamb-like eyes, "What?"

"Was pretty good fight, wa'n't it?"

"Yes," said the youth shortly. He quickened his pace.

But the other hobbled industriously after him. There was an air of apology in his manner, but he evidently thought that he needed only to talk for a time, and the youth would perceive that he was a good fellow.

"Was pretty good fight, wa'n't it?" he began in a small voice, and then he achieved the fortitude to continue. "Dern me if I ever see fellers fight so. Laws, how they did fight! I knowed th' boys 'd like when they onct got square at it. Th' boys ain't had no fair chanct up t' now, but this time they showed what they was. I knowed it 'd turn out this way. Yeh can't lick them boys. No, sir! They're fighters, they be."

He breathed a deep breath of humble admiration. He had looked at the youth for encouragement several times. He received none, but gradually he seemed to get absorbed in his subject.

"I was talkin' 'cross pickets with a boy from Georgie, onct, an' that boy, he ses, 'Your fellers 'll all run like hell when they onct hearn a gun,' he ses. 'Mebbe they will,' I ses, 'but I don't b'lieve none of it,' I ses; 'an' b'jiminey,' I ses back t' 'um, 'mebbe your fellers 'll all run like hell when they onct hearn a gun,' I ses. He larfed. Well, they didn't run t'-day, did they, hey? No, sir! They fit, an' fit, an' fit."

His homely face was suffused with a light of love for the army which was to him all things beautiful and powerful.

After a time he turned to the youth. "Where yeh hit, ol' boy?" he asked in a brotherly tone.

The youth felt instant panic at this question, although at first its full import was not borne in upon him.

"What?" he asked.

"Where yeh hit?" repeated the tattered man.

"Why," began the youth, "I—I—that is— why—I—"

He turned away suddenly and slid through the crowd. His brow was heavily flushed, and his fingers were picking nervously at one of his buttons. He bent his head and fastened his eyes studiously upon the button as if it were a little problem.

The tattered man looked after him in astonishment.

CHAPTER IX

THE youth fell back in the procession until the tattered soldier was not in sight. Then he started to walk on with the others.

But he was amid wounds. The mob of men was bleeding. Because of the tattered soldier's question he now felt that his shame could be viewed. He was continually casting sidelong glances to see if the men were contemplating the letters of guilt he felt burned into his brow.

At times he regarded the wounded soldiers in an envious way. He conceived persons with torn bodies to be peculiarly happy. He wished that he, too, had a wound, a red badge of courage.

The spectral soldier was at his side like a stalking reproach. The man's eyes were still fixed in a stare into the unknown. His gray, appalling face had attracted attention in the crowd, and men, slowing to his dreary pace, were walking with him. They were discussing his plight, questioning him and giving him advice. In a dogged way he repelled them, signing to them to go on and leave him alone. The shadows of his face were deepening and his tight lips seemed holding in check the moan of great despair. There could be seen a certain stiffness in the movements of his body, as if he were taking infinite care not to arouse the passion of his wounds. As he went on, he seemed always looking for a place, like one who goes to choose a grave.

Something in the gesture of the man as he waved the bloody and pitying soldiers away made the youth start as if bitten. He yelled in horror. Tottering forward he laid a quivering hand upon the man's arm. As the latter slowly turned his waxlike features toward him, the youth screamed:

"Gawd! Jim Conklin!"

The tall soldier made a little commonplace smile. "Hello, Henry," he said.

The youth swayed on his legs and glared strangely. He stuttered and stammered. "Oh, Jim—oh, Jim—oh, Jim . . ."

The tall soldier held out his gory hand. There was a curious red and black combination of new blood and old blood upon it. "Where yeh been,

Henry?" he asked. He continued in a monotonous voice, "I thought mebbe yeh got keeled over. There's been thunder t' pay t'-day. I was worryin' about it a good deal."

The youth still lamented. "Oh, Jim—oh, Jim—oh, Jim . . ."

"Yeh know," said the tall soldier, "I was out there." He made a careful gesture. "An', Lord, what a circus! An', b'jiminey, I got shot—I got shot. Yes, b'jiminey, I got shot." He reiterated this fact in a bewildered way, as if he did not know how it came about.

The youth put forth anxious arms to assist him, but the tall soldier went firmly on as if propelled. Since the youth's arrival as a guardian for his friend, the other wounded men had ceased to display much interest. They occupied themselves again in dragging their own tragedies toward the rear.

Suddenly, as the two friends marched on, the tall soldier seemed to be overcome by a terror. His face turned to a semblance of gray paste. He clutched the youth's arm and looked all about him, as if dreading to be overheard. Then he began to speak in a shaking whisper.

"I tell yeh what I'm 'fraid of, Henry—I'll tell

yeh what I'm 'fraid of. I'm 'fraid I'll fall down—
an' then yeh know—them damned artillery wagons—they like as not 'll run over me. That's what
I'm 'fraid of . . ."

The youth cried out to him hysterically: "I'll
take care of yeh, Jim! I'll take care of yeh! I swear
t' Gawd I will!"

"Sure—will yeh, Henry?" the tall soldier
beseeched.

"Yes—yes—I tell yeh—I'll take care of yeh,
Jim!" protested the youth. He could not speak
accurately because of the gulpings in his throat.

But the tall soldier continued to beg in a lowly
way. He now hung babelike to the youth's arm.
His eyes rolled in the wildness of his terror. "I
was allus a good friend t' yeh, wa'n't I, Henry?
I've allus been a pretty good feller, ain't I? An'
it ain't much t' ask, is it? Jest t' pull me along
outer th' road? I'd do it fer you, wouldn't I,
Henry?"

He paused in piteous anxiety to await his
friend's reply.

The youth had reached an anguish where the
sobs scorched him. He strove to express his loy-
alty, but he could only make fantastic gestures.

However, the tall soldier seemed suddenly to

forget all those fears. He became again the grim, stalking specter of a soldier. He went stonily forward. The youth wished his friend to lean upon him, but the other always shook his head and strangely protested. "No—no—no—leave me be—leave me be . . ."

His look was fixed again upon the unknown. He moved with mysterious purpose, and all of the youth's offers he brushed aside. "No—no—leave me be—leave me be . . ."

The youth had to follow.

Presently the latter heard a voice talking softly near his shoulder. Turning he saw that it belonged to the tattered soldier. "Ye'd better take 'im outa th' road, pardner. There's a batt'ry comin' helitywhoop down th' road an' he'll git runned over. He's a goner anyhow in about five minutes—yeh kin see that. Ye'd better take 'im outa th' road. Where th' blazes does he git his stren'th from?"

"Lord knows!" cried the youth. He was shaking his hands helplessly.

He ran forward presently and grasped the tall soldier by the arm. "Jim! Jim!" he coaxed, "come with me."

The tall soldier weakly tried to wrench himself

free. "Huh," he said vacantly. He stared at the youth for a moment. At last he spoke as if dimly comprehending. "Oh! Inteh th' fields? Oh!"

He started blindly through the grass.

The youth turned once to look at the lashing riders and jouncing guns of the battery. He was startled from this view by a shrill outcry from the tattered man.

"Gawd! He's runnin'!"

Turning his head swiftly, the youth saw his friend running in a staggering and stumbling way toward a little clump of bushes. His heart seemed to wrench itself almost free from his body at this sight. He made a noise of pain. He and the tattered man began a pursuit. There was a singular race.

When he overtook the tall soldier he began to plead with all the words he could find. "Jim—Jim—what are you doing—what makes you do this way—you'll hurt yerself."

The same purpose was in the tall soldier's face. He protested in a dulled way, keeping his eyes fastened on the mystic place of his intentions. "No—no—don't tech me—leave me be—leave me be . . ."

The youth, aghast and filled with wonder at

the tall soldier, began quaveringly to question him. "Where yeh goin', Jim? What you thinking about? Where you going? Tell me, won't you, Jim?"

The tall soldier faced about as upon relentless pursuers. In his eyes there was a great appeal. "Leave me be, can't yeh? Leave me be for a minnit."

The youth recoiled. "Why, Jim," he said, in a dazed way, "what's the matter with you?"

The tall soldier turned and, lurching dangerously, went on. The youth and the tattered soldier followed, sneaking as if whipped, feeling unable to face the stricken man if he should again confront them. They began to have thoughts of a solemn ceremony. There was something ritelike in these movements of the doomed soldier. And there was a resemblance in him to a devotee of a mad religion, blood-sucking, muscle-wrenching, bone-crushing. They were awed and afraid. They hung back lest he have at command a dreadful weapon.

At last, they saw him stop and stand motionless. Hastening up, they perceived that his face wore an expression telling that he had at last found the place for which he had struggled. His spare figure was erect; his bloody hands were quietly at his side. He was waiting with patience for something that he had come to meet. He was at the rendezvous. They paused and stood, expectant.

There was a silence.

Finally, the chest of the doomed soldier began to heave with a strained motion. It increased in violence until it was as if an animal was within and was kicking and tumbling furiously to be free.

This spectacle of gradual strangulation made the youth writhe, and once as his friend rolled his eyes, he saw something in them that made him sink wailing to the ground. He raised his voice in a last supreme call.

"Jim—Jim—Jim . . ."

The tall soldier opened his lips and spoke. He made a gesture. "Leave me be—don't tech me—leave me be . . ."

There was another silence while he waited.

Suddenly, his form stiffened and straightened. Then it was shaken by a prolonged ague. He stared into space. To the two watchers there was a curious and profound dignity in the firm lines of his awful face.

He was invaded by a creeping strangeness that slowly enveloped him. For a moment the tremor of his legs caused him to dance a sort of hideous hornpipe. His arms beat wildly about his head in expression of implike enthusiasm.

His tall figure stretched itself to its full height. There was a slight rending sound. Then it began to swing forward, slow and straight, in the manner of a falling tree. A swift muscular contortion made the left shoulder strike the ground first.

The body seemed to bounce a little way from the earth. "God!" said the tattered soldier.

The youth had watched, spellbound, this ceremony at the place of meeting. His face had been twisted into an expression of every agony he had imagined for his friend.

He now sprang to his feet and, going closer, gazed upon the pastelike face. The mouth was open and the teeth showed in a laugh.

As the flap of the blue jacket fell away from the body, he could see that the side looked as if it had been chewed by wolves.

The youth turned, with sudden, livid rage, toward the battlefield. He shook his fist. He seemed about to deliver a philippic.

"Hell . . ."

The red sun was pasted in the sky like a wafer.

CHAPTER X

THE tattered man stood musing.

"Well, he was reg'lar jim-dandy fer nerve, wa'n't he," said he finally in a little awe-struck voice. "A reg'lar jim-dandy." He thoughtfully poked one of the docile hands with his foot. "I wonner where he got 'is stren'th from? I never seen a man do like that before. It was a funny thing. Well, he was a reg'lar jim-dandy."

The youth desired to screech out his grief.

He was stabbed, but his tongue lay dead in the tomb of his mouth. He threw himself again upon the ground and began to brood.

The tattered man stood musing.

"Look-a-here, pardner," he said, after a time. He regarded the corpse as he spoke. "He's up an' gone, ain't 'e, an' we might as well begin t' look out fer ol' number one. This here thing is all over. He's up an' gone, ain't 'e? An' he's all right here. Nobody won't bother 'im. An' I must say I ain't enjoying any great health m'self these days."

The youth, awakened by the soldier's tone, looked quickly up. He saw that he was swinging uncertainly on his legs and that his face had turned to a shade of blue.

"Good Lord!" he cried, "you ain't goin' t'—not you, too."

The tattered man waved his hand. "Nary die," he said. "All I want is some pea soup an' a good bed. Some pea soup," he repeated dreamfully.

The youth arose from the ground. "I wonder where he came from. I left him over there." He pointed. "And now I find 'im here. And he was coming from over there, too." He indicated a new direction. They both turned toward the body as if to ask it a question.

"Well," at length spoke the tattered man, "there ain't no use in our stayin' here an' tryin' t' ask him anything."

The youth nodded an assent wearily. They both turned to gaze for a moment at the corpse.

The youth murmured something.

"Well, he was a jim-dandy, wa'n't 'e?" said the tattered man as if in response.

They turned their backs upon it and started away. For a time they stole softly, treading with their toes. It remained laughing there in the grass.

"I'm commencin' t' feel pretty bad," said the tattered man, suddenly breaking one of his little silences. "I'm commencin' t' feel pretty damn' bad."

The youth groaned. "O Lord!" He wondered if he was to be the tortured witness of another grim encounter.

But his companion waved his hand reassuringly. "Oh, I'm not goin' t' die yit! There's too much dependin' on me fer me t' die yit. No, sir! Nary die; I *can't*! Ye'd oughta see th' swad a' chil'ren I've got, an' all like that."

The youth glancing at his companion could see by the shadow of a smile that he was making some kind of fun.

As they plodded on the tattered soldier continued to talk. "Besides, if I died, I wouldn't die th' way that feller did. That was th' funniest thing. I'd jest flop down, I would. I never seen a feller die th' way that feller did.

"Yeh know Tom Jamison, he lives next door t' me up home. He's a nice feller, he is, an' we was allus good friends. Smart, too. Smart as a steel trap. Well, when we was a-fightin' this afternoon, all-of-a-sudden he begin t' rip up an' cuss an' beller at me. 'Yer shot, yeh blamed infernal!'—he swear horrible—he ses t' me. I put m' hand t' m' head an' when I looked at m' fingers, I seen, sure 'nough, I was shot. I give a holler an' begin t' run, but b'fore I could git away another one hit me in th' arm an' whirl' me clean 'round. I got skeared when they was all a-shootin' b'hind me an' I run t' beat all, but I cotch it pretty bad. I've an idee I'd a' been fightin' yit, if t'wasn't fer Tom Jamison."

Then he made a calm announcement: "There's two of 'em—little ones—but they're beginnin' t' have fun with me now. I don't b'lieve I kin walk much furder."

They went slowly on in silence. "Yeh look pretty peek-ed yerself," said the tattered man at last. "I bet yeh've got a worser one than yeh think. Ye'd better take keer of yer hurt. It don't do t' let sech things go. It might be inside mostly, an' them plays thunder. Where is it located?" But he continued his harangue without waiting for a reply. "I see' a feller git hit plum in th' head when my reg'ment was a-standin' at ease onct. An' everybody yelled out to 'im: 'Hurt, John? Are yeh hurt much?' 'No,' ses he. He looked kinder surprised, an' he went on tellin' 'em how he felt. He sed he didn't feel nothin'. But, by dad, th' first thing that feller knowed he was dead. Yes, he was dead—stone dead. So, yeh wanta watch out. Yeh might have some queer kind 'a hurt yerself. Yeh can't never tell. Where is your'n located?"

The youth had been wriggling since the introduction of this topic. He now gave a cry of exasperation and made a furious motion with his hand. "Oh, don't bother me!" he said. He was enraged against the tattered man, and could have strangled him. His companions seemed ever to play intolerable parts. They were ever upraising the ghost of shame on the stick of their curiosity. He turned toward the tattered man as one at bay. "Now, don't bother me," he repeated with desperate menace.

"Well, Lord knows I don't wanta bother anybody," said the other. There was a little accent of despair in his voice as he replied, "Lord knows I've gota 'nough m' own t' tend to."

The youth, who had been holding a bitter debate with himself and casting glances of hatred and contempt at the tattered man, here spoke in a hard voice. "Good-by," he said.

The tattered man looked at him in gaping amazement. "Why—why, pardner, where yeh goin'?" he asked unsteadily. The youth looking at him, could see that he, too, like that other one, was beginning to act dumb and animal-like. His thoughts seemed to be floundering about in his head. "Now—now—look—a—here, you Tom Jamison—now—I won't have this—this here won't do. Where—where yeh goin'?"

The youth pointed vaguely. "Over there," he replied.

"Well, now look—a—here—now," said the tattered man, rambling on in idiot fashion. His head was hanging forward and his words were slurred. "This thing won't do, now, Tom Jamison. It won't do. I know yeh, yeh pig-headed devil. Yeh wanta go trompin' off with a bad hurt. It ain't right—now—Tom Jamison—it ain't. Yeh wanta leave me take keer of yeh, Tom Jamison. It ain't—right—it ain't—fer yeh t' go—trompin' off—with a bad hurt—it ain't—ain't—ain't right—it ain't."

In reply the youth climbed a fence and started away. He could hear the tattered man bleating plaintively.

Once he faced about angrily. "What?"

"Look—a—here, now, Tom Jamison—now—it ain't—"

The youth went on. Turning at a distance he saw the tattered man wandering about helplessly in the field.

He now thought that he wished he was dead. He believed that he envied those men whose bodies lay strewn over the grass of the fields and on the fallen leaves of the forest.

The simple questions of the tattered man had been knife thrusts to him. They asserted a society that probes pitilessly at secrets until all is apparent. His late companion's chance persistency made him feel that he could not keep his crime concealed in his bosom. It was sure to be brought plain by one of those arrows which cloud the air and are constantly pricking, discovering, proclaiming those things which are willed to be forever hidden. He admitted that he could not defend himself against this agency. It was not within the power of vigilance.

CHAPTER XI

H E became aware that the furnace roar of the battle was growing louder. Great brown clouds had floated to the still heights of air before him. The noise, too, was approaching. The woods filtered men and the fields became dotted.

As he rounded a hillock, he perceived that the roadway was now a crying mass of wagons, teams, and men. From the heaving tangle issued exhortations, commands, imprecations. Fear was sweeping it all along. The cracking whips bit and horses plunged and tugged. The white-topped wagons strained and stumbled in their exertions like fat sheep.

The youth felt comforted in a measure by this sight. They were all retreating. Perhaps, then, he was not so bad after all. He seated himself and watched the terror-stricken wagons. They fled like soft, ungainly animals. All the roarers and lashers served to help him to magnify the dangers and horrors of the engagement that he might try to prove to himself that the thing with which men could charge him was in truth a symmetrical act. There was an amount of pleasure to him in watching the wild march of this vindication.

Presently the calm head of a forward-going column of infantry appeared in the road. It came swiftly on. Avoiding the obstructions gave it the sinuous movement of a serpent. The men at the head butted mules with their musket stocks. They prodded teamsters indifferent to all howls. The men forced their way through parts of the dense mass by strength. The blunt head of the column pushed. The raving teamsters swore many strange oaths.

The commands to make way had the ring of a great importance in them. The men were going forward to the heart of the din. They were to confront the eager rush of the enemy. They felt the pride of their onward movement when the remainder of the army seemed trying to dribble down this road. They tumbled teams about with a fine feeling that it was no matter so long as their column got to the front in time. This importance made their faces grave and stern. And the backs of the officers were very rigid.

As the youth looked at them the black weight of his woe returned to him. He felt that he was regarding a procession of chosen beings. The separation was as great to him as if they had marched with weapons of flame and banners of sunlight. He could never be like them. He could have wept in his longings.

He searched about in his mind for an adequate malediction for the indefinite cause, the thing upon which men turn the words of final blame. It—whatever it was—was responsible for him, he said. There lay the fault.

The haste of the column to reach the battle seemed to the forlorn young man to be something much finer than stout fighting. Heroes, he thought, could find excuses in that long seething lane. They could retire with perfect self-respect and make excuses to the stars.

He wondered what those men had eaten that they could be in such haste to force their way to grim chances of death. As he watched, his envy grew until he thought that he wished to change lives with one of them. He would have liked to have used a tremendous force, he said, throw off himself and become a better. Swift pictures of himself, apart, yet in himself, came to him—a blue desperate figure leading lurid charges with one knee forward and a broken blade high—a blue, determined figure standing before a crimson and steel assault, getting calmly killed on a high place before the eyes of all. He thought of the magnificent pathos of his dead body.

These thoughts uplifted him. He felt the quiver of war desire. In his ears, he heard the ring of victory. He knew the frenzy of a rapid successful charge. The music of the trampling feet, the sharp voices, the clanking arms of the column near him made him soar on the red wings of war. For a few moments he was sublime.

He thought that he was about to start for the front. Indeed, he saw a picture of himself, dust-stained, haggard, panting, flying to the front at the proper moment to seize and throttle the dark, leering witch of calamity.

Then the difficulties of the thing began to drag at him. He hesitated, balancing awkwardly on one foot.

He had no rifle; he could not fight with his

hands, said he resentfully to his plan. Well, rifles could be had for the picking. They were extraordinarily profuse.

Also, he continued, it would be a miracle if he found his regiment. Well, he could fight with any regiment.

He started forward slowly. He stepped as if he expected to tread upon some explosive thing. Doubts and he were struggling.

He would truly be a worm if any of his comrades should see him returning thus, the marks of his flight upon him. There was a reply that the intent fighters did not care for what happened rearward saving that no hostile bayonets appeared there. In the battle-blur his face would, in a way, be hidden, like the face of a cowled man.

But then he said that his tireless fate would bring forth, when the strife lulled for a moment, a man to ask of him an explanation. In imagination he felt the scrutiny of his companions as he painfully labored through some lies.

Eventually, his courage expended itself upon these objections. The debates drained him of his fire.

He was not cast down by this defeat of his plan, for, upon studying the affair carefully, he could not but admit that the objections were very formidable.

Furthermore, various ailments had begun to cry out. In their presence he could not persist in flying high with the wings of war; they rendered it almost impossible for him to see himself in a heroic light. He tumbled headlong.

He discovered that he had a scorching thirst. His face was so dry and grimy that he thought he could feel his skin crackle. Each bone of his body had an ache in it, and seemingly threatened to break with each movement. His feet were like two sores. Also, his body was calling for food. It was more powerful than a direct hunger. There was a dull, weight-like feeling in his stomach, and, when he tried to walk, his head swayed and he tottered. He could not see with distinctness. Small patches of green mist floated before hls vision.

While he had been tossed by many emotions, he had not been aware of ailments. Now they beset him and made clamor. As he was at last compelled to pay attention to them, his capacity for self-hate was multiplied. In despair, he declared that he was not like those others. He now conceded it to be impossible that he should ever become a hero. He was a craven loon. Those pictures of glory were piteous things. He groaned from his heart and went staggering off.

A certain mothlike quality within him kept him in the vicinity of the battle. He had a great desire to see, and to get news. He wished to know who was winning.

He told himself that, despite his unprecedented suffering, he had never lost his greed for a victory, yet, he said, in a half-apologetic manner to his conscience, he could not but know that a defeat for the army this time might mean many favorable things for him. The blows of the enemy would splinter regiments into fragments. Thus, many men of courage, he considered, would be obliged to desert the colors and scurry like chickens. He would appear as one of them. They would be sullen brothers in distress, and he could then easily believe he had not run any farther or faster than they. And if he himself could believe in his virtuous perfection, he conceived that there would be small trouble in convincing all others.

He said, as if in excuse for this hope, that previously the army had encountered great defeats and in a few months had shaken off all blood and tradition of them, emerging as bright and valiant as a new one; thrusting out of sight the memory

of disaster, and appearing with the valor and confidence of unconquered legions. The shrilling
voices of the people at home would pipe dismally
for a time, but various generals were usually
compelled to listen to these ditties. He of course
felt no compunctions for proposing a general as
a sacrifice. He could not tell who the chosen for
the barbs might be, so he could center no direct
sympathy upon him. The people were afar and
he did not conceive public opinion to be accurate
at long range. It was quite probable they would
hit the wrong man who, after he had recovered
from his amazement, would perhaps spend the
rest of his days in writing replies to the songs of
his alleged failure. It would be very unfortunate,
no doubt, but in this case a general was of no
consequence to the youth.

In a defeat there would be a roundabout vindication of himself. He thought it would prove,
in a manner, that he had fled early because of his
superior powers of perception. A serious prophet
upon predicting a flood should be the first man
to climb a tree. This would demonstrate that he
was indeed a seer.

A moral vindication was regarded by the youth
as a very important thing. Without salve, he

could not, he thought, wear the sore badge of his dishonor through life. With his heart continually assuring him that he was despicable, he could not exist without making it, through his actions, apparent to all men.

If the army had gone gloriously on he would be lost. If the din meant that now his army's flags were tilted forward he was a condemned wretch. He would be compelled to doom himself to isolation. If the men were advancing, their indifferent feet were trampling upon his chances for a successful life.

As these thoughts went rapidly through his mind, he turned upon them and tried to thrust them away. He denounced himself as a villain. He said that he was the most unutterably selfish man in existence. His mind pictured the soldiers who would place their defiant bodies before the spear of the yelling battle fiend, and as he saw their dripping corpses on an imagined field, he said that he was their murderer.

Again he thought that he wished he was dead. He believed that he envied a corpse. Thinking of the slain, he achieved a great contempt for some of them, as if they were guilty for thus becoming lifeless. They might have been killed by lucky chances, he said, before they had had opportunities to flee or before they had been really tested. Yet they would receive laurels from tradition. He cried out bitterly that their crowns were stolen and their robes of glorious memories were shams. However, he still said that it was a great pity he was not as they.

A defeat of the army had suggested itself to him as a means of escape from the consequences of his fall. He considered, now, however, that it was useless to think of such a possibility. His education had been that success for that mighty blue machine was certain; that it would make victories as a contrivance turns out buttons. He presently discarded all his speculations in the other direction. He returned to the creed of soldiers.

When he perceived again that it was not possible for the army to be defeated, he tried to bethink him of a fine tale which he could take back to his regiment, and with it turn the expected shafts of derision.

But, as he mortally feared these shafts, it became impossible for him to invent a tale he felt he could trust. He experimented with many schemes, but threw them aside one by one as flimsy. He was quick to see vulnerable places in them all.

Furthermore, he was much afraid that some arrow of scorn might lay him mentally low before he could raise his protecting tale.

He imagined the whole regiment saying: "Where's Henry Fleming? He run, didn't 'e? Oh, my!" He recalled various persons who would be quite sure to leave him no peace about it. They would doubtless question him with sneers, and laugh at his stammering hesitation. In the next engagement they would try to keep watch of him to discover when he would run.

Wherever he went in camp, he would encounter insolent and lingeringly cruel stares. As he imagined himself passing near a crowd of comrades, he could hear some one say, "There he goes!"

Then, as if the heads were moved by one muscle, all the faces were turned toward him with wide, derisive grins. He seemed to hear some one make a humorous remark in a low tone. At it the others all crowed and cackled. He was a slang phrase.

CHAPTER XII

THE column that had butted stoutly at the obstacles in the roadway was barely out of the youth's sight before he saw dark waves of men come sweeping out of the woods and down through the fields. He knew at once that the steel fibers had been washed from their hearts. They were bursting from their coats and their equipments as from entanglements. They charged down upon him like terrified buffaloes.

Behind them blue smoke curled and clouded above the treetops, and through the thickets he could sometimes see a distant pink glare. The voices of the cannon were clamoring in interminable chorus.

The youth was horror-stricken. He stared in agony and amazement. He forgot that he was engaged in combating the universe. He threw aside his mental pamphlets on the philosophy of the retreated and rules for the guidance of the damned.

The fight was lost. The dragons were coming with invincible strides. The army, helpless in the matted thickets and blinded by the overhanging night, was going to be swallowed. War, the red animal, war, the blood-swollen god, would have bloated fill.

Within him something bade to cry out. He had the impulse to make a rallying speech, to sing a battle hymn, but he could only get his tongue to call into the air: "Why—why—what—what's th' matter?"

Soon he was in the midst of them. They were leaping and scampering all about him. Their blanched faces shone in the dusk. They seemed, for the most part, to be very burly men. The youth turned from one to another of them as they galloped along. His incoherent questions were lost. They were heedless of his appeals. They did not seem to see him.

They sometimes gabbled insanely. One huge man was asking of the sky: "Say, where de plank road? Where de plank road!" It was as if he had lost a child. He wept in his pain and dismay.

Presently, men were running hither and thither

in all ways. The artillery booming, forward, rearward, and on the flanks made jumble of ideas of direction. Landmarks had vanished into the gathered gloom. The youth began to imagine that he had got into the center of the tremendous quarrel, and he could perceive no way out of it. From the mouths of the fleeing men came a thousand wild questions, but no one made answers.

The youth, after rushing about and throwing interrogations at the heedless bands of retreating infantry, finally clutched a man by the arm. They swung around face to face.

"Why—why . . ." stammered the youth struggling with his balking tongue.

The man screamed: "Let go me! Let go me!" His face was livid and his eyes were rolling uncontrolled. He was heaving and panting. He still grasped his rifle, perhaps having forgotten to release his hold upon it. He tugged frantically, and the youth being compelled to lean forward was dragged several paces.

"Let go me! Let go me!"

"Why—why . . ." stuttered the youth.

"Well, then!" bawled the man in a lurid rage. He adroitly and fiercely swung his rifle. It crushed upon the youth's head. The man ran on.

The youth's fingers had turned to paste upon the other's arm. The energy was smitten from his muscles. He saw the flaming wings of lightning flash before his vision. There was a deafening rumble of thunder within his head.

Suddenly his legs seemed to die. He sank writhing to the ground. He tried to arise. In his efforts against the numbing pain he was like a man wrestling with a creature of the air.

There was a sinister struggle.

Sometimes he would achieve a position half erect, battle with the air for a moment, and then fall again, grabbing at the grass. His face was of a clammy pallor. Deep groans were wrenched from him.

As last, with a twisting movement, he got upon his hands and knees, and from thence, like a babe trying to walk, to his feet. Pressing his hands to his temples he went lurching over the grass.

He fought an intense battle with his body. His dulled senses wished him to swoon and he opposed them stubbornly, his mind portraying unknown dangers and mutilations if he should fall upon the field. He went tall soldier fashion. He imagined secluded spots where he could fall and be unmolested. To search for one he strove against the tide of his pain.

Once he put his hand to the top of his head and timidly touched the wound. The scratching pain of the contact made him draw a long breath through his clinched teeth. His fingers were dabbled with blood. He regarded them with a fixed stare.

Around him he could hear the grumble of jolted cannon as the scurrying horses were lashed toward the front. Once, a young officer on a besplashed charger nearly ran him down. He turned and watched the mass of guns, men, and horses sweeping in a wide curve toward a gap in a fence. The officer was making excited motions with a gauntleted hand. The guns followed the teams with an air of unwillingness, of being dragged by the heels.

Some officers of the scattered infantry were cursing and railing like fishwives. Their scolding voices could be heard above the din. Into the unspeakable jumble in the roadway rode a squadron of cavalry. The faded yellow of their facings shone bravely. There was a mighty altercation.

The artillery were assembling as if for a conference.

The blue haze of evening was upon the field. The lines of forest were long purple shadows. One cloud lay along the western sky partly smothering the red.

As the youth left the scene behind him, he heard the guns suddenly roar out. He imagined them shaking in black rage. They belched and howled like brass devils guarding a gate. The soft air was filled with the tremendous remonstrance. With it came the shattering peal of opposing infantry. Turning to look behind him, he could see sheets of orange light illumine the shadowy distance. There were subtle and sudden lightnings in the far air. At times he thought he could see heaving masses of men.

He hurried on in the dusk. The day had faded until he could barely distinguish place for his feet. The purple darkness was filled with men who lectured and jabbered. Sometimes he could see them gesticulating against the blue and somber sky. There seemed to be a great ruck of men and munitions spread about in the forest and in the fields.

The little narrow roadway now lay lifeless. There were overturned wagons like sun-dried bowlders. The bed of the former torrent was choked with the bodies of horses and splintered parts of war machines.

It had come to pass that his wound pained him but little. He was afraid to move rapidly, however, for a dread of disturbing it. He held his head very still and took many precautions against stumbling. He was filled with anxiety, and his face was pinched and drawn in anticipation of the pain of any sudden mistake of his feet in the gloom.

His thoughts, as he walked, fixed intently upon his hurt. There was a cool, liquid feeling about it and he imagined blood moving slowly down under his hair. His head seemed swollen to a size that made him think his neck to be inadequate.

The new silence of his wound made much worriment. The little blistering voices of pain that had called out from his scalp were, he thought, definite in their expression of danger. By them he believed that he could measure his plight. But when they remained ominously silent he became frightened and imagined terrible fingers that clutched into his brain.

Amid it he began to reflect upon various incidents and conditions of the past. He bethought him of certain meals his mother had cooked at home, in which those dishes of which he was particularly fond had occupied prominent positions. He saw the spread table. The pine walls of the kitchen were glowing in the warm light from the stove. Too, he remembered how he and his companions used to go from the schoolhouse to the bank of a shaded pool. He saw his clothes in disorderly array upon the grass of the bank. He felt the swash of the fragrant water upon his body. The leaves of the overhanging maple rustled with melody in the wind of youthful summer.

He was overcome presently by a dragging weariness. His head hung forward and his shoulders were stooped as if he were bearing a great bundle. His feet shuffled along the ground.

He held continuous arguments as to whether he should lie down and sleep at some near spot, or force himself on until he reached a certain haven. He often tried to dismiss the question, but his body persisted in rebellion and his senses nagged at him like pampered babies.

At last he heard a cheery voice near his shoulder: "Yeh seem t' be in a pretty bad way, boy?"

The youth did not look up, but he assented with thick tongue, "Uh!"

The owner of the cheery voice took him firmly by the arm. "Well," he said, with a round laugh, "I'm goin' your way. Th' hull gang is goin' your way. An' I guess I kin give yeh a lift." They began to walk like a drunken man and his friend.

As they went along, the man questioned the youth and assisted him with the replies like one manipulating the mind of a child. Sometimes he interjected anecdotes. "What reg'ment do yeh b'long teh? Eh? What's that? Th' 304th N' York? Why, what corps is that in? Oh, it is? Why, I thought they wasn't engaged t'-day— they're 'way over in th' center. Oh, they was, eh? Well, pretty nearly everybody got their share 'a fightin' t'-day. By dad, I give myself up fer dead any number 'a times. There was shootin' here an' shootin' there, an' hollerin' here an' hollerin' there, in th' damn' darkness, until I couldn't tell t' save m' soul which side I was on. Sometimes I thought I was sure 'nough from Ohier, an' other times I could a' swore I was from th' bit- ter end of Florida. It was th' most mixed up dern thing I ever see. An' these here hull woods is a reg'lar mess. It'll be a miracle if we find our reg'ment t'-night. Pretty soon, though, we'll meet a-plenty of guards an' provost-guards, an' one thing an' another. Ho! there they go with an off'cer, I guess. Look at his hand a-draggin'. He's got all th' war he wants, I bet. He won't be talkin' so big about his reputation an' all when they go t' sawin' off his leg. Poor feller! My brother's got whiskers jest like that. How did yeh git 'way over here, anyhow? Your reg'ment is a long way from here, ain't it? Well, I guess we can find it. Yeh know there was a boy killed in my comp'ny t'-day that I thought th' world an' all of. Jack was a nice feller. By ginger, it hurt like thunder t' see ol' Jack jest git knocked flat. We was a-standin' purty peaceable for a spell, 'though there was men runnin' ev'ry way all 'round us, an' while we was a-standin' like that, 'long come a big fat feller. He began t' peck at Jack's elbow, an' he ses: 'Say, where 's th' road t' th' river?' An' Jack, he never paid no attention, an' th' feller kept on a-peckin' at his elbow an' sayin': 'Say, where's th' road t' th' river?' Jack was a-lookin' ahead all th' time tryin' t' see th' Johnnies comin' through th' woods, an' he never paid no attention t' this big fat feller fer a long time, but at last he turned 'round an' he ses: 'Ah, go t' hell an' find th' road t' th' river!' An' jest then a shot slapped him bang on th' side th' head. He was a sergeant, too. Them was his last words. Thunder, I wish we was sure 'a findin' our reg'ments t'-night. It's goin' t' be long huntin'. But I guess we kin do it."

In the search which followed, the man of the cheery voice seemed to the youth to possess a wand of a magic kind. He threaded the mazes of the tangled forest with a strange fortune. In encounter with guards and patrols he displayed the keenness of a detective and the valor of a gamin. Obstacles fell before him and became of assistance. The youth, with his chin still on his breast, stood woodenly by while his companion beat ways and means out of sullen things.

The forest seemed a vast hive of men buzzing about in frantic circles, but the cheery man conducted the youth without mistakes until at last he began to chuckle with glee and self-satisfaction. "Ah, there yeh are! See that fire?"

The youth nodded stupidly.

"Well, there's where your reg'ment is. An' now, good-by, ol' boy, good luck t' yeh."

A warm and strong hand clasped the youth's languid fingers for an instant, and then he heard a cheerful and audacious whistling as the man strode away. As he who had so befriended him was thus passing out of his life, it suddenly occurred to the youth that he had not once seen his face.

CHAPTER XIII

THE youth went slowly toward the fire indicated by his departed friend. As he reeled, he bethought him of the welcome his comrades would give him. He had a conviction that he would soon feel in his sore heart the barbed missiles of ridicule. He had no strength to invent a tale; he would be a soft target.

He made vague plans to go off into the deeper darkness and hide, but they were all destroyed by the voices of exhaustion and pain from his body. His ailments, clamoring, forced him to seek the place of food and rest, at whatever cost.

He swung unsteadily toward the fire. He could see the forms of men throwing black shadows in the red light, and as he went nearer it became known to him in some way that the ground was strewn with sleeping men.

Of a sudden he confronted a black and monstrous figure. A rifle barrel caught some glinting beams. "Halt! halt!" He was dismayed for a moment, but he presently thought that he recognized the nervous voice. As he stood tottering before the rifle barrel, he called out: "Why, hello, Wilson, you—you here?"

The rifle was lowered to a position of caution and the loud soldier came slowly forward. He peered into the youth's face. "That you, Henry?"

"Yes, it's—it's me."

"Well, well, ol' boy," said the other, "by ginger, I'm glad t' see yeh! I give yeh up fer a goner. I thought yeh was dead sure enough." There was husky emotion in his voice.

The youth found that now he could barely stand upon his feet. There was a sudden sinking of his forces. He thought he must hasten to produce his tale to protect him from the missiles already at the lips of his redoubtable comrades. So, staggering before the loud soldier, he began: "Yes, yes. I've—I've had an awful time. I've been all over. Way over on th' right. Ter'ble fightin' over there. I had an awful time. I got separated from th' reg'ment. Over on th' right, I got shot. In th' head. I never see sech fightin'. Awful time.

I don't see how I could a' got separated from th' reg'ment. I got shot, too."

His friend had stepped forward quickly. "What? Got shot? Why didn't yeh say so first? Poor ol' boy, we must—hol' on a minnit; what am I doin'? I'll call Simpson."

Another figure at that moment loomed in the gloom. They could see that it was the corporal. "Who yeh talkin' to, Wilson?" he demanded. His voice was anger-toned. "Who yeh talkin' to? Yeh th' derndest sentinel—why—hello, Henry, you here? Why, I thought you was dead four hours ago! Great Jerusalem, they keep turnin' up every ten minutes or so! We thought we'd lost forty-two men by straight count, but if they keep on a-comin' this way, we'll git th' comp'ny all back by mornin' yit. Where was yeh?"

"Over on th' right. I got separated"—began the youth with considerable glibness.

But his friend had interrupted hastily. "Yes, an' he got shot in th' head an' he's in a fix, an' we must see t' him right away." He rested his rifle in the hollow of his left arm and his right around the youth's shoulder.

"Gee, it must hurt like thunder!" he said.

The youth leaned heavily upon his friend. "Yes, it hurts—hurts a good deal," he replied. There was a faltering in his voice.

"Oh," said the corporal. He linked his arm in the youth's and drew him forward. "Come on, Henry. I'll take keer 'a yeh."

As they went on together the loud private called out after them: "Put 'im t' sleep in my blanket, Simpson. An'—hol' on a minnit—here's my canteen. It's full 'a coffee. Look at his head by th' fire an' see how it looks. Maybe it's a pretty bad un. When I git relieved in a couple 'a minnits, I'll be over an' see t' him." The youth's senses were so deadened that his friend's voice sounded from afar and he could scarcely feel the pressure of the corporal's arm. He submitted passively to the latter's directing strength. His head was in the old manner hanging forward upon his breast. His knees wobbled.

The corporal led him into the glare of the fire. "Now, Henry," he said, "let's have look at yer ol' head."

The youth sat down obediently and the corporal, laying aside his rifle, began to fumble in the bushy hair of his comrade. He was obliged to turn the other's head so that the full flush of the fire light would beam upon it. He puckered his mouth with a critical air. He drew back his lips and whistled through his teeth when his fingers came in contact with the splashed blood and the rare wound.

"Ah, here we are!" he said. He awkwardly made further investigations. "Jest as I thought," he added, presently. "Yeh've been grazed by a ball. It's raised a queer lump jest as if some feller had lammed yeh on th' head with a club. It stopped a-bleedin' long time ago. Th' most about it is that in th' mornin' yeh'll feel that a number ten hat wouldn't fit yeh. An' your head 'll be all het up an' feel as dry as burnt pork. An' yeh may git a lot 'a other sicknesses, too, by mornin'. Yeh can't never tell. Still, I don't much think so. It's jest a damn' good belt on th' head, an' nothin' more. Now, you jest sit here an' don't move, while I go rout out th' relief. Then I'll send Wilson t' take keer 'a yeh."

The corporal went away. The youth remained on the ground like a parcel. He stared with a vacant look into the fire.

After a time he aroused, for some part, and the things about him began to take form. He saw that the ground in the deep shadows was cluttered with men, sprawling in every conceivable posture. Glancing narrowly into the more distant darkness, he caught occasional glimpses of visages that loomed pallid and ghostly, lit with a phosphorescent glow. These faces expressed in their lines the deep stupor of the tired soldiers. They made them appear like men drunk with wine. This bit of forest might have appeared to an ethereal wanderer as a scene of the result of some frightful debauch.

On the other side of the fire the youth observed an officer asleep, seated bolt upright, with his back against a tree. There was something perilous in his position. Badgered by dreams, perhaps, he swayed with little bounces and starts, like an old, toddy-stricken grandfather in a chimney corner. Dust and stains were upon his face. His lower jaw hung down as if lacking strength to assume its normal position. He was the picture of an exhausted soldier after a feast of war.

He had evidently gone to sleep with his sword in his arms. These two had slumbered in an embrace, but the weapon had been allowed in time to fall unheeded to the ground. The brass-mounted hilt lay in contact with some parts of the fire.

Within the gleam of rose and orange light from the burning sticks were other soldiers, snoring and heaving, or lying deathlike in slumber. A few pairs of legs were stuck forth, rigid and straight. The shoes displayed the mud or dust of marches and bits of rounded trousers, protruding from the blankets, showed rents and tears from hurried pitchings through the dense brambles.

The fire crackled musically. From it swelled light smoke. Overhead the foliage moved softly. The leaves, with their faces turned toward the blaze, were colored shifting hues of silver, often edged with red. Far off to the right, through a window in the forest, could be seen a handful of stars lying, like glittering pebbles, on the black level of the night.

Occasionally, in this low-arched hall, a soldier would arouse and turn his body to a new position, the experience of his sleep having taught him of uneven and objectionable places upon the ground under him. Or, perhaps, he would lift himself to a sitting posture, blink at the fire for an unintelligent moment, throw a swift glance at his prostrate companion, and then cuddle down again with a grunt of sleepy content.

The youth sat in a forlorn heap until his

friend, the loud young soldier, came, swinging two canteens by their light strings. "Well, now, Henry, ol' boy," said the latter, "we'll have yeh fixed up in jest about a minnit."

He had the bustling ways of an amateur nurse. He fussed around the fire and stirred the sticks to brilliant exertions. He made his patient drink largely from the canteen that contained the coffee. It was to the youth a delicious draught. He tilted his head afar back and held the canteen long to his lips. The cool mixture went caressingly down his blistered throat. Having finished, he sighed with comfortable delight.

The loud young soldier watched his comrade with an air of satisfaction. He later produced an extensive handkerchief from his pocket. He folded it into a manner of bandage and soused water from the other canteen upon the middle of it. This crude arrangement he bound over the youth's head, tying the ends in a queer knot at the back of the neck.

"There," he said, moving off and surveying his deed, "yeh look like th' devil, but I bet yeh feel better."

The youth contemplated his friend with grateful eyes. Upon his aching and swelling head the cold cloth was like a tender woman's hand.

"Yeh don't holler ner say nothin'," remarked his friend approvingly. "I know I'm a blacksmith at takin' keer 'a sick folks, an' yeh never squeaked. Yer a good un, Henry. Most 'a men would 'a been in th' hospital long ago. A shot in th' head ain't foolin' business."

The youth made no reply, but began to fumble with the buttons of his jacket.

"Well, come, now," continued his friend, "come on. I must put yeh t' bed an' see that yeh git a good night's rest."

The other got carefully erect, and the loud young soldier led him among the sleeping forms lying in groups and rows. Presently he stooped and picked up his blankets. He spread the rubber one upon the ground and placed the woolen one about the youth's shoulders.

"There now," he said, "lie down an' git some sleep."

The youth, with his manner of doglike obedience, got carefully down like a crone stooping. He stretched out with a murmur of relief and comfort. The ground felt like the softest couch.

But of a sudden he ejaculated: "Hol' on a minnit! Where you goin' t' sleep?"

His friend waved his hand impatiently. "Right
down there by yeh."

"Well, but hol' on a minnit," continued the
youth. "What yeh goin' t' sleep in? I've got
your . . ."

The loud young soldier snarled: "Shet up an'
go on t' sleep. Don't be makin' a damn' fool 'a
yerself," he said severely.

After the reproof the youth said no more. An
exquisite drowsiness had spread through him.
The warm comfort of the blanket enveloped him
and made a gentle languor. His head fell forward
on his crooked arm and his weighted lids went
slowly down over his eyes. Hearing a splatter of
musketry from the distance, he wondered indif-
ferently if those men sometimes slept. He gave a
long sigh, snuggled down into his blanket, and
in a moment was like his comrades.

CHAPTER XIV

WHEN the youth awoke it seemed to him that he had been asleep for a thousand years, and he felt sure that he opened his eyes upon an unexpected world. Gray mists were slowly shifting before the first efforts of the sun-rays. An impending splendor could be seen in the eastern sky. An icy dew had chilled his face, and immediately upon arousing he curled farther down into his blankets. He stared for a while at the leaves overhead, moving in a heraldic wind of the day.

The distance was splintering and blaring with the noise of fighting. There was in the sound an expression of a deadly persistency, as if it had not begun and was not to cease.

About him were the rows and groups of men that he had dimly seen the previous night. They were getting a last draught of sleep before the awakening. The gaunt, careworn features and dusty figures were made plain by this quaint light at the dawning, but it dressed the skin of the men in corpselike hues and made the tangled limbs appear pulseless and dead. The youth started up with a little cry when his eyes first swept over this motionless mass of men, thick-spread upon the ground, pallid, and in strange postures. His disordered mind interpreted the hall of the forest as a charnel place. He believed for a instant that he was in the house of the dead, and he did not dare to move lest these corpses start up, squalling and squawking. In a second, however, he achieved his proper mind. He swore a complicated oath at himself. He saw that this somber picture was not a fact of the present, but a mere prophecy.

He heard then the noise of a fire crackling briskly in the cold air, and, turning his head, he saw his friend pottering busily about a small blaze. A few other figures moved in the fog, and he heard the hard cracking of axe blows.

Suddenly there was a hollow rumble of drums. A distant bugle sang faintly. Similar sounds, varying in strength, came from near and far over the forest.

The bugles called to each other like brazen gamecocks. The near thunder of the regimental drums rolled.

The body of men in the woods rustled. There was a general uplifting of heads. A murmuring of voices broke upon the air. In it there was much bass of grumbling oaths. Strange gods were addressed in condemnation of the early hours necessary to correct war. An officer's peremptory tenor rang out and quickened the stiffened movement of the men. The tangled limbs unraveled. The corpse-hued faces were hidden behind fists that twisted slowly in the eye sockets.

The youth sat up and gave vent to an enormous yawn. "Thunder!" he remarked petulantly. He rubbed his eyes, and then putting up his hand felt carefully of the bandage over his wound. His friend, perceiving him to be awake, came from the fire. "Well, Henry, ol' man, how do yeh feel this mornin'?" he demanded.

The youth yawned again. Then he puckered his mouth to a little pucker. His head, in truth, felt precisely like a melon, and there was an unpleasant sensation at his stomach.

"Oh, Lord, I feel pretty bad," he said.

"Thunder!" exclaimed the other. "I hoped ye'd

feel all right this mornin'. Let's see th' bandage—
I guess it's slipped." He began to tinker at the
wound in rather a clumsy way until the youth
exploded.

"Gosh-dern it!" he said in sharp irritation:
"you're the hangdest man I ever saw! You wear
muffs on your hands. Why in good thunderation
can't you be more easy? I'd rather you'd stand off
an' throw guns at it. Now, go slow, an' don't act
as if you was nailing down carpet."

He glared with insolent command at his
friend, but the latter answered soothingly.
"Well, well, come now, an' git some grub," he
said. "Then, maybe, yeh'll feel better."

At the fireside the loud young soldier watched
over his comrade's wants with tenderness and
care. He was very busy marshaling the little black
vagabonds of tin cups and pouring into them the
streaming, iron colored mixture from a small and
sooty tin pail. He had some fresh meat, which he
roasted hurriedly upon a stick. He sat down then
and contemplated the youth's appetite with glee.

The youth took note of a remarkable change in
his comrade since those days of camp life upon
the river bank. He seemed no more to be continually regarding the proportions of his personal

prowess. He was not furious at small words that pricked his conceits. He was no more a loud young soldier. There was about him now a fine reliance. He showed a quiet belief in his purposes and his abilities. And this inward confidence evidently enabled him to be indifferent to little words of other men aimed at him.

The youth reflected. He had been used to regarding his comrade as a blatant child with an audacity grown from his inexperience, thoughtless, headstrong, jealous, and filled with a tinsel courage. A swaggering babe accustomed to strut in his own dooryard. The youth wondered where had been born these new eyes; when his comrade had made the great discovery that there were many men who would refuse to be subjected by him. Apparently, the other had now climbed a peak of wisdom from which he could perceive himself as a very wee thing. And the youth saw that ever after it would be easier to live in his friend's neighborhood.

His comrade balanced his ebony coffee cup on his knee. "Well, Henry," he said, "what d'yeh think th' chances are? D'yeh think we'll wallop 'em?"

The youth considered for a moment. "Day

b'fore-yesterday," he finally replied, with bold-ness, "you would 'a' bet you'd lick the hull kit-an'-boodle all by yourself."

His friend looked a trifle amazed. "Would I?" he asked. He pondered. "Well, perhaps I would," he decided at last. He stared humbly at the fire.

The youth was quite disconcerted at this sur-prising reception of his remarks. "Oh, no, you wouldn't either," he said, hastily trying to retrace.

But the other made a deprecating gesture. "Oh, yeh needn't mind, Henry," he said. "I believe I was a pretty big fool in those days." He spoke as after a lapse of years.

There was a little pause.

"All th' officers say we've got th' rebs in a pretty tight box," said the friend, clearing his throat in a commonplace way. "They all seem t' think we've got 'em jest where we want 'em."

"I don't know about that," the youth replied. "What I seen over on th' right makes me think it was th' other way about. From where I was, it looked as if we was gettin' a good poundin' yestirday."

"D'yeh think so?" inquired the friend. "I thought we handled 'em pretty rough yestirday."

"Not a bit," said the youth. "Why, lord, man, you didn't see nothing of the fight. Why!" Then a sudden thought came to him. "Oh! Jim Conklin's dead."

His friend started. "What? Is he? Jim Conklin?"

The youth spoke slowly. "Yes. He's dead. Shot in th' side."

"Yeh don't say so. Jim Conklin . . . poor cuss!"

All about them were other small fires surrounded by men with their little black utensils. From one of these near came sudden sharp voices in a row. It appeared that two light-footed soldiers had been teasing a huge, bearded man, causing him to spill coffee upon his blue knees. The man had gone into a rage and had sworn comprehensively. Stung by his language, his tormentors had immediately bristled at him with a great show of resenting unjust oaths. Possibly there was going to be a fight.

The friend arose and went over to them, making pacific motions with his arms. "Oh, here, now, boys, what's th' use?" he said. "We'll be at th' rebs in less'n an hour. What's th' good fightin' 'mong ourselves?"

One of the light-footed soldiers turned upon

him red-faced and violent. "Yeh needn't come around here with yer preachin'. I s'pose yeh don't approve 'a fightin' since Charley Morgan licked yeh; but I don't see what business this here is 'a yours or anybody else."

"Well, it ain't," said the friend mildly. "Still I hate t' see . . ."

That was a tangled argument.

"Well, he . . . ," said the two, indicating their opponent with accusative forefingers.

The huge soldier was quite purple with rage. He pointed at the two soldiers with his great hand, extended clawlike. "Well, they . . ."

But during this argumentative time the desire to deal blows seemed to pass, although they said much to each other. Finally the friend returned to his old seat.

In a short while the three antagonists could be seen together in an amiable bunch.

"Jimmie Rogers ses I'll have t' fight him after th' battle t'-day," announced the friend as he again seated himself. "He ses he don't allow no interferin' in his business. I hate t' see th' boys fightin' 'mong themselves."

The youth laughed. "Yer changed a good bit. Yeh ain't at all like yeh was. I remember when you an' that Irish feller . . ." He stopped and laughed again.

"No, I didn't use t' be that way," said his friend thoughtfully. "That's true 'nough."

"Well, I didn't mean . . ." began the youth.

The friend made another deprecatory gesture. "Oh, yeh needn't mind, Henry."

There was another little pause.

"Th' reg'ment lost over half th' men yestirday," remarked the friend eventually. "I thought 'a course they was all dead, but, laws, they kep' a-comin' back last night until it seems, after all, we didn't lose but a few. They'd been scattered all over, wanderin' around in th' woods, fightin' with other reg'ments, an' everything. Jest like you done."

"So?" said the youth.

CHAPTER XV

THE regiment was standing at order arms at the side of a lane, waiting for the command to march, when suddenly the youth remembered the little packet enwrapped in a faded yellow envelope which the loud young soldier with lugubrious words had intrusted to him. It made him start. He uttered an exclamation and turned toward his comrade.

"Wilson!"

His friend, at his side in the ranks, was thoughtfully staring down the road. From some cause his expression was at that moment very meek. The youth, regarding him with sidelong glances, felt impelled to change his purpose. "Oh, nothin'," he said.

His friend turned his head in some surprise, "Why, what was yeh goin' t' say?"

"Oh, nothin," repeated the youth.

He resolved not to deal the little blow. It was sufficient that the fact made him glad. It was not necessary to knock his friend on the head with the misguided packet.

He had been possessed of much fear of his friend, for he saw how easily questionings could make holes in his feelings. Lately, he had assured himself that the altered comrade would not tantalize him with a persistent curiosity, but he felt certain that during the first period of leisure his friend would ask him to relate his adventures of the previous day.

He now rejoiced in the possession of a small weapon with which he could prostrate his comrade at the first signs of a cross-examination. He was master. It would now be he who could laugh and shoot the shafts of derision.

The friend had, in a weak hour, spoken with sobs of his own death. He had delivered a melancholy oration previous to his funeral, and had doubtless, in the packet of letters, presented various keepsakes to relatives. But he had not died, and thus he had delivered himself into the hands of the youth.

The latter felt immensely superior to his friend, but he inclined to condescension. He adopted toward him an air of patronizing good humor.

His self-pride was now entirely restored. In the shade of its flourishing growth he stood with braced and self-confident legs, and since nothing could now be discovered he did not shrink from an encounter with the eyes of judges, and allowed no thoughts of his own to keep him from an attitude of manfulness. He had performed his mistakes in the dark, so he was still a man.

Indeed, when he remembered his fortunes of yesterday, and looked at them from a distance he began to see something fine there. He had license to be pompous and veteranlike.

His panting agonies of the past he put out of his sight.

In the present, he declared to himself that it was only the doomed and the damned who roared with sincerity at circumstance. Few but they ever did it. A man with a full stomach and the respect of his fellows had no business to scold about anything that he might think to be wrong in the ways of the universe, or even with the ways of society. Let the unfortunates rail; the others may play marbles.

He did not give a great deal of thought to

these battles that lay directly before him. It was not essential that he should plan his ways in regard to them. He had been taught that many obligations of a life were easily avoided. The lessons of yesterday had been that retribution was a laggard and blind. With these facts before him he did not deem it necessary that he should become feverish over the possibilities of the ensuing twenty-four hours. He could leave much to chance. Besides, a faith in himself had secretly blossomed. There was a little flower of confidence growing within him. He was now a man of experience. He had been out among the dragons, he said, and he assured himself that they were not so hideous as he had imagined them. Also, they were inaccurate; they did not sting with precision. A stout heart often defied, and, defying, escaped.

And, furthermore, how could they kill him who was the chosen of gods and doomed to greatness?

He remembered how some of the men had run from the battle.

As he recalled their terror-struck faces he felt a scorn for them. They had surely been more fleet and more wild than was absolutely necessary. They were weak mortals. As for himself, he had fled with discretion and dignity.

He was aroused from this reverie by his friend, who, having hitched about nervously and blinked at the trees for a time, suddenly coughed in an introductory way, and spoke.

"Fleming!"

"What?"

The friend put his hand up to his mouth and coughed again. He fidgeted in his jacket.

"Well," he gulped, at last, "I guess yeh might as well give me back them letters." Dark, prickling blood had flushed into his cheeks and brow.

"All right, Wilson," said the youth. He loosened two buttons of his coat, thrust in his hand, and brought forth the packet. As he extended it to his friend the latter's face was turned from him.

He had been slow in the act of producing the packet because during it he had been trying to invent a remarkable comment upon the affair. He could conjure nothing of sufficient point. He was compelled to allow his friend to escape unmolested with his packet. And for this he took unto himself considerable credit. It was a generous thing.

His friend at his side seemed suffering great shame. As he contemplated him, the youth felt his heart grow more strong and stout. He had never been compelled to blush in such manner for his acts; he was an individual of extraordinary virtues.

He reflected, with condescending pity: "Too bad! Too bad! The poor devil, it makes him feel tough!"

After this incident, and as he reviewed the battle pictures he had seen, he felt quite competent to return home and make the hearts of the people glow with stories of war. He could see himself in a room of warm tints telling tales to listeners. He could exhibit laurels. They were insignificant; still, in a district where laurels were infrequent, they might shine.

He saw his gaping audience picturing him as the central figure in blazing scenes. And he imagined the consternation and the ejaculations of his mother and the young lady at the seminary as they drank his recitals. Their vague feminine formula for beloved ones doing brave deeds on the field of battle without risk of life would be destroyed.

CHAPTER XVI

A sputtering of musketry was always to be heard. Later, the cannon had entered the dispute. In the fog-filled air their voices made a thudding sound. The reverberations were continual. This part of the world led a strange, battleful existence.

The youth's regiment was marched to relieve a command that had lain long in some damp trenches. The men took positions behind a curving line of rifle pits that had been turned up, like a large furrow, along the line of woods. Before them was a level stretch, peopled with short, deformed stumps. From the woods beyond came the dull popping of the skirmishers and pickets, firing in the fog. From the right came the noise of a terrific fracas.

The men cuddled behind the small embankment and sat in easy attitudes awaiting their turn.

Many had their backs to the firing. The youth's friend lay down, buried his face in his arms, and almost instantly, it seemed, he was in a deep sleep.

The youth leaned his breast against the brown dirt and peered over at the woods and up and down the line. Curtains of trees interfered with his ways of vision. He could see the low line of trenches but for a short distance. A few idle flags were perched on the dirt hills. Behind them were rows of dark bodies with a few heads sticking curiously over the top.

Always the noise of skirmishers came from the woods on the front and left, and the din on the right had grown to frightful proportions. The guns were roaring without an instant's pause for breath. It seemed that the cannon had come from all parts and were engaged in a stupendous wrangle. It became impossible to make a sentence heard.

The youth wished to launch a joke—a quotation from newspapers. He desired to say, "All quiet on the Rappahannock," but the guns refused to permit even a comment upon their uproar. He never successfully concluded the sentence. But at last the guns stopped, and among

the men in the rifle pits rumors again flew, like
birds, but they were now for the most part black
creatures who flapped their wings drearily near to
the ground and refused to rise on any wings of
hope. The men's faces grew doleful from the
interpreting of omens. Tales of hesitation and
uncertainty on the part of those high in place and
responsibility came to their ears. Stories of disaster were borne into their minds with many
proofs. This din of musketry on the right, growing like a released genie of sound, expressed and
emphasized the army's plight.

The men were disheartened and began to mutter. They made gestures expressive of the sentence: "Ah, what more can we do?" And it could
always be seen that they were bewildered by the
alleged news and could not fully comprehend a
defeat.

Before the gray mists had been totally obliter-
ated by the sun rays, the regiment was marching
in a spread column that was retiring carefully
through the woods. The disordered, hurrying
lines of the enemy could sometimes be seen down
through the groves and little fields. They were
yelling, shrill and exultant.

At this sight the youth forgot many personal

matters and became greatly enraged. He exploded in loud sentences. "B'jiminey, we're generaled by a lot 'a lunkheads."

"More than one feller has said that t'-day," observed a man.

His friend, recently aroused, was still very drowsy. He looked behind him until his mind took in the meaning of the movement. Then he sighed. "Oh, well, I s'pose we got licked," he remarked sadly.

The youth had a thought that it would not be handsome for him to freely condemn other men. He made an attempt to restrain himself, but the words upon his tongue were too bitter. He presently began a long and intricate denunciation of the commander of the forces.

"Mebbe, it wa'n't all his fault—not all together. He did th' best he knowed. It's our luck t' git licked often," said his friend in a weary tone. He was trudging along with stooped shoulders and shifting eyes like a man who has been caned and kicked.

"Well, don't we fight like the devil? Don't we do all that men can?" demanded the youth loudly.

He was secretly dumbfounded at this sentiment when it came from his lips. For a moment his face lost its valor and he looked guiltily about him. But no one questioned his right to deal in such words, and presently he recovered his air of courage. He went on to repeat a statement he had heard going from group to group at the camp that morning. "The brigadier said he never saw a new reg'ment fight the way we fought yestir-day, didn't he? And we didn't do better than any another reg'ment, did we? Well, then, you can't say it's th' army's fault, can you?"

In his reply, the friend's voice was stern. " 'A course not," he said. "No man dare say we don't fight like th' devil. No man will ever dare say it. Th' boys fight like hell-roosters. But still—still, we don't have no luck."

"Well, then, if we fight like the devil an' don't ever whip, it must be the general's fault," said the youth grandly and decisively. "And I don't see any sense in fighting and fighting and fight-ing, yet always losing through some derned old lunkhead of a general."

A sarcastic man who was tramping at the youth's side, then spoke lazily. "Mebbe yeh think yeh fit th' hull battle yestirday, Fleming," he remarked.

The speech pierced the youth. Inwardly he was reduced to an abject pulp by these chance words. His legs quaked privately. He cast a frightened glance at the sarcastic man.

"Why, no," he hastened to say in a conciliating voice, "I don't think I fought the whole battle yesterday."

But the other seemed innocent of any deeper meaning. Apparently, he had no information. It was merely his habit. "Oh!" he replied in the same tone of calm derision.

The youth, nevertheless, felt a threat. His mind shrank from going nearer to the danger, and thereafter he was silent. The significance of the sarcastic man's words took from him all loud moods that would make him appear prominent. He became suddenly a modest person.

There was low-toned talk among the troops. The officers were impatient and snappy, their countenances clouded with the tales of misfortune. The troops, sifting through the forest, were sullen. In the youth's company once a man's laugh rang out. A dozen soldiers turned their faces quickly toward him and frowned with vague displeasure.

The noise of firing dogged their footsteps.

Sometimes, it seemed to be driven a little way, but it always returned again with increased insolence. The men muttered and cursed, throwing black looks in its direction.

In a clear space the troops were at last halted. Regiments and brigades, broken and detached through their encounters with thickets, grew together again and lines were faced toward the pursuing bark of the enemy's infantry.

This noise, following like the yelpings of eager, metallic hounds, increased to a loud and joyous burst, and then, as the sun went serenely up the sky, throwing illuminating rays into the gloomy thickets, it broke forth into prolonged pealings. The woods began to crackle as if afire.

"Whoop-a-dadee," said a man, "here we are! Everybody fightin'. Blood an' destruction."

"I was willin' t' bet they'd attack as soon as th' sun got fairly up," savagely asserted the lieutenant who commanded the youth's company. He jerked without mercy at his little mustache. He strode to and fro with dark dignity in the rear of his men, who were lying down behind whatever protection they had collected.

A battery had trundled into position in the rear and was thoughtfully shelling the distance. The

regiment, unmolested as yet, awaited the moment
when the gray shadows of the woods before them
should be slashed by the lines of flame. There
was much growling and swearing.

"Good Gawd," the youth grumbled, "we're
always being chased around like rats! It makes me
sick. Nobody seems to know where we go or why
we go. We just get fired around from pillar to
post and get licked here and get licked there, and
nobody knows what it's done for. It makes a man
feel like a damn' kitten in a bag. Now, I'd like to
know what the eternal thunders we was marched
into these woods for anyhow, unless it was to give
the rebs a regular pot shot at us. We came in here
and got our legs all tangled up in these cussed
briers, and then we begin to fight and the rebs
had an easy time of it. Don't tell me it's just luck!
I know better. It's this derned old . . ."

The friend seemed jaded, but he interrupted
his comrade with a voice of calm confidence.
"It'll turn out all right in th' end," he said.

"Oh, the devil it will! You always talk like a
dog-hanged parson. Don't tell me! I know . . ."

At this time there was an interposition by the
savage-minded lieutenant, who was obliged to
vent some of his inward dissatisfaction upon his

men. "You boys shut right up! There no need 'a your wastin' your breath in long-winded arguments about this an' that an' th' other. You've been jawin' like a lot 'a old hens. All you've got t' do is to fight, an' you'll get plenty 'a that t' do in about ten minutes. Less talkin' an' more fightin' is what's best for you boys. I never saw sech gabbling jackasses."

He paused, ready to pounce upon any man who might have the temerity to reply. No words being said, he resumed his dignified pacing.

"There's too much chin music an' too little fightin' in this war, anyhow," he said to them, turning his head for a final remark.

The day had grown more white, until the sun shed his full radiance upon the thronged forest. A sort of a gust of battle came sweeping toward that part of the line where lay the youth's regiment. The front shifted a trifle to meet it squarely. There was a wait. In this part of the field there passed slowly the intense moments that precede the tempest.

A single rifle flashed in a thicket before the regiment. In an instant it was joined by many others. There was a mighty song of clashes and crashes that went sweeping through the woods.

The guns in the rear, aroused and enraged by shells that had been thrown burr-like at them, suddenly involved themselves in a hideous altercation with another band of guns. The battle roar settled to a rolling thunder, which was a single long explosion.

In the regiment there was a peculiar kind of hesitation denoted in the attitudes of the men. They were worn, exhausted, having slept but little and labored much. They rolled their eyes toward the advancing battle as they stood awaiting the shock. Some shrank and flinched. They stood as men tied to stakes.

CHAPTER XVII

THIS advance of the enemy had seemed to the youth like a ruthless hunting. He began to fume with rage and exasperation. He beat his foot upon the ground, and scowled with hate at the swirling smoke that was approaching like a phantom flood. There was a maddening quality in this seeming resolution of the foe to give him no rest, to give him no time to sit down and think. Yesterday he had fought and had fled rapidly. There had been many adventures. For today he felt that he had earned opportunities for contemplative repose. He could have enjoyed portraying to uninitiated listeners various scenes at which he had been a witness or ably discussing the processes of war with other proved men. Too it was important that he should have time for physical recuperation. He was sore and stiff from his experiences. He had received his fill of all exertions, and he wished to rest.

But those other men seemed never to grow weary; they were fighting with their old speed. He had a wild hate for the relentless foe. Yesterday, when he had imagined the universe to be against him, he had hated it, little gods and big gods; to-day he hated the army of the foe with the same great hatred. He was not going to be badgered of his life, like a kitten chased by boys, he said. It was not well to drive men into final corners; at those moments they could all develop teeth and claws.

He leaned and spoke into his friend's ear. He menaced the woods with a gesture. "If they keep on chasing us, by Gawd, they'd better watch out. Can't stand *too* much."

The friend twisted his head and made a calm reply. "If they keep on a-chasin' us they'll drive us all inteh th' river."

The youth cried out savagely at this statement. He crouched behind a little tree, with his eyes burning hatefully and his teeth set in a curlike snarl. The awkward bandage was still about his head, and upon it, over his wound, there was a

spot of dry blood. His hair was wondrously tousled, and some straggling, moving locks hung over
the cloth of the bandage down toward his fore-
head. His jacket and shirt were open at the throat,
and exposed his young bronzed neck. There could
be seen spasmodic gulpings at his throat.

His fingers twined nervously about his rifle.
He wished that it was an engine of annihilating
power. He felt that he and his companions were
being taunted and derided from sincere convic-
tions that they were poor and puny. His knowledge of his inability to take vengeance for it made
his rage into a dark and stormy specter, that possessed him and made him dream of abominable
cruelties. The tormentors were flies sucking insolently at his blood, and he thought that he would
have given his life for a revenge of seeing their
faces in pitiful plights.

The winds of battle had swept all about the
regiment, until the one rifle, instantly followed by
brothers, flashed in its front. A moment later the
regiment roared forth its sudden and valiant
retort. A dense wall of smoke settled slowly
down. It was furiously slit and slashed by the
knifelike fire from the rifles.

To the youth the fighters resembled animals tossed for a death struggle into a dark pit. There was a sensation that he and his fellows, at bay, were pushing back, always pushing fierce onslaughts of creatures who were slippery. Their beams of crimson seemed to get no purchase upon the bodies of their foes; the latter seemed to evade them with ease, and come through, between, around, and about with unopposed skill.

When, in a dream, it occurred to the youth that his rifle was an impotent stick, he lost sense of everything but his hate, his desire to smash into pulp the glittering smile of victory which he could feel upon the faces of his enemies.

The blue smoke-swallowed line curled and writhed like a snake stepped upon. It swung its ends to and fro in an agony of fear and rage.

The youth was not conscious that he was erect upon his feet. He did not know the direction of the ground. Indeed, once he even lost the habit of balance and fell heavily. He was up again immediately. One thought went through the chaos of his brain at the time. He wondered if he had fallen because he had been shot. But the sus-

picion flew away at once. He did not think more
of it.

He had taken up a first position behind the little tree, with a direct determination to hold it
against the world. He had not deemed it possible that his army could that day succeed, and
from this he felt the ability to fight harder. But
the throng had surged in all ways, until he lost
directions and locations, save that he knew where
lay the enemy.

The flames bit him, and the hot smoke broiled
his skin. His rifle barrel grew so hot that ordi-
narily he could not have borne it upon his palms;
but he kept on stuffing cartridges into it, and
pounding them with his clanking, bending ram-
rod. If he aimed at some changing form through
the smoke, he pulled his trigger with a fierce
grunt, as if he were dealing a blow of the fist with
all his strength.

When the enemy seemed falling back before
him and his fellows, he went instantly forward,
like a dog who, seeing his foes lagging, turns and
insists upon being pursued. And when he was
compelled to retire again, he did it slowly, sullenly, taking steps of wrathful despair.

Once he, in his intent hate, was almost alone, and was firing, when all those near him had ceased. He was so engrossed in his occupation that he was not aware of a lull.

He was recalled by a hoarse laugh and a sentence that came to his ears in a voice of contempt and amazement. "Yeh infernal fool, don't yeh know enough t' quit when there ain't anything t' shoot at? Good Gawd!"

He turned then and, pausing with his rifle thrown half into position, looked at the blue line of his comrades. During this moment of leisure they seemed all to be engaged in staring with astonishment at him. They had become spectators. Turning to the front again he saw, under the lifted smoke, a deserted ground.

He looked bewildered for a moment. Then there appeared upon the glazed vacancy of his eyes a diamond point of intelligence. "Oh," he said, comprehending.

He returned to his comrades and threw himself upon the ground. He sprawled like a man who had been thrashed. His flesh seemed strangely on fire, and the sounds of the battle continued in his ears. He groped blindly for his canteen.

The lieutenant was crowing. He seemed drunk
with fighting. He called out to the youth: "By
heavens, if I had ten thousand wild cats like you
I could tear th' stomach outa this war in less'n a
week!" He puffed out his chest with large dignity as he said it.

Some of the men muttered and looked at the
youth in awe-struck ways. It was plain that as he
had gone on loading and firing and cursing without the proper intermission, they had found time
to regard him. And they now looked upon him as
a war devil.

The friend came staggering to him. There was
some fright and dismay in his voice. "Are yeh all
right, Fleming? Do yeh feel all right? There ain't
nothin' th' matter with yeh, Henry, is there?"

"No," said the youth with difficulty. His
throat seemed full of knobs and burrs.

These incidents made the youth ponder. It was
revealed to him that he had been a barbarian, a
beast. He had fought like a pagan who defends
his religion. Regarding it, he saw that it was fine,
wild, and, in some ways, easy. He had been a
tremendous figure, no doubt. By this struggle he
had overcome obstacles which he had admitted to

be mountains. They had fallen like paper peaks, and he was now what he called a hero. And he had not been aware of the process. He had slept and, awakening, found himself a knight.

He lay and basked in the occasional stares of his comrades. Their faces were varied in degrees of blackness from the burned powder. Some were utterly smudged. They were reeking with perspiration, and their breaths came hard and wheezing. And from these soiled expanses they peered at him.

"Hot work! Hot work!" cried the lieutenant deliriously. He walked up and down, restless and eager. Sometimes his voice could be heard in a wild, incomprehensible laugh.

When he had a particularly profound thought upon the science of war he always unconsciously addressed himself to the youth.

There was some grim rejoicing by the men. "By thunder, I bet this army'll never see another new reg'ment like us!"

"You bet!

"A dog, a woman, an' a walnut tree,
Th' more yeh beat 'em, th' better they be!

That's like us."

"Lost a piler men, they did. If an ol' woman swep' up th' woods she'd git a dustpanful."

"Yes, an' if she'll come around ag'in in 'bout an hour she'll git a pile more."

The forest still bore its burden of clamor. From off under the trees came the rolling clatter of the musketry. Each distant thicket seemed a strange porcupine with quills of flame. A cloud of dark smoke, as from smoldering ruins, went up toward the sun now bright and gay in the blue, enameled sky.

CHAPTER XVIII

THE ragged line had respite for some minutes, but during its pause the struggle in the forest became magnified until the trees seemed to quiver from the firing and the ground to shake from the rushing of the men. The voices of the cannon were mingled in a long and interminable row. It seemed difficult to live in such an atmosphere. The chests of the men strained for a bit of freshness, and their throats craved water.

There was one shot through the body, who raised a cry of bitter lamentation when came this lull. Perhaps he had been calling out during the fighting also, but at that time no one had heard him. But now the men turned at the woeful complaints of him upon the ground.

"Who is it? Who is it?"

"It's Jimmie Rogers. Jimmie Rogers."

When their eyes first encountered him there

was a sudden halt, as if they feared to go near. He was thrashing about in the grass, twisting his shuddering body into many strange postures. He was screaming loudly. This instant's hesitation seemed to fill him with a tremendous, fantastic contempt, and he damned them in shrieked sentences.

The youth's friend had a geographical illusion concerning a stream, and he obtained permission to go for some water. Immediately canteens were showered upon him. "Fill mine, will yeh?" "Bring me some, too." "And me, too." He departed, laden. The youth went with his friend, feeling a desire to throw his heated body into the stream and, soaking there, drink quarts.

They made a hurried search for the supposed stream, but did not find it. "No water here," said the youth. They turned without delay and began to retrace their steps.

From their position as they again faced toward the place of the fighting, they could of course comprehend a greater amount of the battle than when their visions had been blurred by the hurling smoke of the line. They could see dark stretches winding along the land, and on one cleared space there was a row of guns making gray clouds, which were filled with large flashes of orange-colored flame. Over some foliage they could see the roof of a house. One window, glowing a deep murder red, shone squarely through the leaves. From the edifice a tall leaning tower of smoke went far into the sky.

Looking over their own troops, they saw mixed masses slowly getting into regular form. The sunlight made twinkling points of the bright steel. To the rear there was a glimpse of a distant roadway as it curved over a slope. It was crowded with retreating infantry. From all the interwoven forest arose the smoke and bluster of the battle. The air was always occupied by a blaring.

Near where they stood shells were flip-flapping and hooting. Occasional bullets buzzed in the air and spanged into tree trunks. Wounded men and other stragglers were slinking through the woods.

Looking down an aisle of the grove, the youth and his companion saw a jangling general and his staff almost ride upon a wounded man who was crawling on his hands and knees. The general reined strongly at his charger's opened and foamy mouth and guided it with dexterous horsemanship past the man. The latter scrambled in wild and torturing haste. His strength evidently failed him as he reached a place of safety. One of his arms suddenly weakened, and he fell, sliding over upon his back. He lay stretched out, breathing gently.

A moment later the small, creaking cavalcade was directly in front of the two soldiers. Another officer, riding with the skillful abandon of a cowboy, galloped his horse to a position directly before the general. The two unnoticed foot soldiers made a little show of going on, but they lingered near in the desire to overhear the conversation. Perhaps, they thought, some great inner historical things would be said.

The general, whom the boys knew as the commander of their division, looked at the other officer and spoke coolly, as if he were criticising his clothes. "Th' enemy's formin' over there for another charge," he said. "It'll be directed against Whiterside, an' I fear they'll break through there unless we work like thunder t' stop them."

The other swore at his restive horse, and then cleared his throat. He made a gesture toward his cap. "It'll be hell t' pay stoppin' them," he said shortly.

"I presume so," remarked the general. Then he began to talk rapidly and in a lower tone. He fre-

quently illustrated his words with a pointing finger. The two infantrymen could hear nothing
until finally he asked: "What troops can you
spare?"

The officer who rode like a cowboy reflected
for an instant. "Well," he said, "I had to order in
th' 12th to help th' 76th, an' I haven't really got
any. But there's th' 304th. They fight like a lot 'a
mule drivers. I can spare them best of any."

The youth and his friend exchanged glances of
astonishment.

The general spoke sharply. "Get 'em ready,
then. I'll watch developments from here, an' send
you word when t' start them. It'll happen in five
minutes."

As the other officer tossed his fingers toward
his cap and, wheeling his horse, started away, the
general called out to him in a sober voice: "I don't
believe many of your mule drivers will get back."

The other shouted something in reply. He
smiled.

With scared faces, the youth and his companion hurried back to the line.

These happenings had occupied an incredibly
short time, yet the youth felt that in them he had
been made aged. New eyes were given to him.

And the most startling thing was to learn suddenly that he was very insignificant. The officer spoke of the regiment as if he referred to a broom. Some part of the woods needed sweeping, perhaps, and he merely indicated a broom in a tone properly indifferent to its fate. It was war, no doubt, but it appeared strange.

As the two boys approached the line, the lieutenant perceived them and swelled with wrath. "Fleming—Wilson—how long does it take yeh to git water, anyhow—where yeh been to."

But his oration ceased as he saw their eyes, which were large with great tales. "We're goin' t' charge—we're goin' t' charge!" cried the youth's friend, hastening with his news.

"Charge?" said the lieutenant. "Charge? Well, b'Gawd! Now; this is real fightin'." Over his soiled countenance there went a boastful smile. "Charge? Well, b'Gawd!"

A little group of soldiers surrounded the two youths. "Are we, sure 'nough? Well, I'll be derned! Charge? What fer? What at? Wilson, you're lyin'."

"I hope to die," said the youth's friend, pitching his tones to the key of angry remonstrance. "Sure as shooting, I tell you."

And the youth spoke in re-enforcement. "Not by a blame sight, he ain't lyin'. We heard 'em talkin'."

They caught sight of two mounted figures a short distance from them. One was the colonel of the regiment and the other was the officer who had received orders from the commander of the division. They were gesticulating at each other. The soldier, pointing at them, interpreted the scene.

One man had a final objection: "How could yeh hear 'em talkin'?" But the men, for a large part, nodded, admitting that previously the two friends had spoken truth.

They settled back into reposeful attitudes with airs of having accepted the matter. And they mused upon it, with a hundred varieties of expression. It was an engrossing thing to think about. Many tightened their belts carefully and hitched at their trousers.

A moment later the officers began to hustle among the men, pushing them into a more compact mass and into a better alignment. They chased those that straggled and fumed at a few men who seemed to show by their attitudes that they had decided to remain at that spot. They were like critical shepherds struggling with sheep.

Presently, the regiment seemed to draw itself up and heave a deep breath. None of the men's faces were mirrors of large thoughts. The soldiers were bended and stooped like sprinters before a signal. Many pairs of glinting eyes peered from the grimy faces toward the curtains of the deeper woods. They seemed to be engaged in deep calculations of time and distance.

They were surrounded by the noises of the monstrous altercation between the two armies. The world was fully interested in other matters. Apparently, the regiment had its small affair to itself.

The youth, turning, shot a quick, inquiring glance at his friend. The latter returned to him the same manner of look. They were the only ones who possessed an inner knowledge. "Mule drivers—hell t' pay—don't believe many will get back." It was an ironical secret. Still, they saw no hesitation in each other's faces, and they nodded a mute and unprotesting assent when a shaggy man near them said in a meek voice: "We'll git swallowed."

CHAPTER XIX

THE youth stared at the land in front of him. Its foliage now seemed to veil powers and horrors. He was unaware of the machinery of orders that started the charge, although from the corners of his eyes he saw an officer, who looked like a boy a-horseback, come galloping, waving his hat. Suddenly he felt a straining and heaving among the men. The line fell slowly forward like a toppling wall, and, with a convulsive gasp that was intended for a cheer, the regiment began its journey. The youth was pushed and jostled for a moment before he understood the movement at all, but directly he lunged ahead and began to run.

He fixed his eye upon a distant and prominent clump of trees where he had concluded the enemy were to be met, and he ran toward it as toward a goal. He had believed throughout that it was a mere question of getting over an unpleasant matter as quickly as possible, and he ran desperately, as if pursued for a murder. His face was drawn hard and tight with the stress of his endeavor. His eyes were fixed in a lurid glare. And with his soiled and disordered dress, his red and inflamed features surmounted by the dingy rag with its spot of blood, his wildly swinging rifle and banging accouterments, he looked to be an insane soldier.

As the regiment swung from its position out into a cleared space the woods and thickets before it awakened. Yellow flames leaped toward it from many directions. The forest made a tremendous objection.

The line lurched straight for a moment. Then the right wing swung forward; it in turn was surpassed by the left. Afterward the center careered to the front until the regiment was a wedge-shaped mass, but an instant later the opposition of the bushes, trees, and uneven places on the ground split the command and scattered it into detached clusters.

The youth, light-footed, was unconsciously in advance. His eyes still kept note of the clump of trees. From all places near it the clannish yell of the enemy could be heard. The little flames of rifles leaped from it. The song of the bullets was in the air and shells snarled among the tree-tops. One tumbled directly into the middle of a hurrying group and exploded in crimson fury. There was an instant's spectacle of a man, almost over it, throwing up his hands to shield his eyes.

Other men, punched by bullets, fell in grotesque agonies. The regiment left a coherent trail of bodies.

They had passed into a clearer atmosphere. There was an effect like a revelation in the new appearance of the landscape. Some men working madly at a battery were plain to them, and the opposing infantry's lines were defined by the gray walls and fringes of smoke.

It seemed to the youth that he saw everything. Each blade of the green grass was bold and clear. He thought that he was aware of every change in the thin, transparent vapor that floated idly in sheets. The brown or gray trunks of the trees showed each roughness of their surfaces. And the men of the regiment, with their starting eyes and sweating faces, running madly, or falling, as if thrown headlong, to queer, heaped-up corpses— all were comprehended. His mind took a mechanical but firm impression, so that afterward everything was pictured and explained to him, save why he himself was there.

But there was a frenzy made from this furious rush. The men, pitching forward insanely, had burst into cheerings, moblike and barbaric, but tuned in strange keys that can arouse the dullard and the stoic. It made a mad enthusiasm that, it seemed, would be incapable of checking itself before granite and brass. There was the delirium that encounters despair and death, and is heedless and blind to the odds. It is a temporary but sublime absence of selfishness. And because it was of this order was the reason, perhaps, why the youth wondered, afterward, what reasons he could have had for being there.

Presently the straining pace ate up the energies of the men. As if by agreement, the leaders began to slacken their speed. The volleys directed against them had had a seeming wind-like effect. The regiment snorted and blew. Among some stolid trees it began to falter and hesitate. The men, staring intently, began to wait for some of the distant walls of smoke to move and disclose to them the scene. Since much of their strength and their breath had vanished, they returned to caution. They were become men again.

The youth had a vague belief that he had run miles, and he thought, in a way, that he was now in some new and unknown land.

The moment the regiment ceased its advance the protesting splutter of musketry became a steadied roar. Long and accurate fringes of smoke spread out. From the top of a small hill came level belchings of yellow flame that caused an inhuman whistling in the air.

The men, halted, had opportunity to see some of their comrades dropping with moans and shrieks. A few lay under foot, still or wailing. And now for an instant the men stood, their rifles slack in their hands, and watched the regiment dwindle. They appeared dazed and stupid. This spectacle seemed to paralyze them, overcome them with a fatal fascination. They stared woodenly at the sights, and, lowering their eyes, looked from face to face. It was a strange pause, and a strange silence.

Then, above the sounds of the outside commotion, arose the roar of the lieutenant. He strode suddenly forth, his infantile features black with rage.

"Come on, yeh fools!" he bellowed. "Come on! Yeh can't stay here. Yeh must come on." He said more, but much of it could not be understood.

He started rapidly forward, with his head turned toward the men. "Come on," he was shouting. The men stared with blank and yokel-like eyes at him. He was obliged to halt and retrace his steps. He stood then with his back to the enemy and delivered gigantic curses into the faces of the men. His body vibrated from the weight and force of his imprecations. And he could string oaths with the facility of a maiden who strings beads.

The friend of the youth aroused. Lurching suddenly forward and dropping to his knees, he fired an angry shot at the persistent woods. This action awakened the men. They huddled no more like sheep. They seemed suddenly to bethink them of their weapons, and at once commenced firing. Belabored by their officers, they began to move forward. The regiment, involved like a cart involved in mud and muddle, started unevenly with many jolts and jerks. The men stopped now every few paces to fire and load, and in this man-ner moved slowly on from trees to trees.

The flaming opposition in their front grew

with their advance until it seemed that all forward ways were barred by the thin leaping
tongues, and off to the right an ominous demonstration could sometimes be dimly discerned.
The smoke lately generated was in confusing
clouds that made it difficult for the regiment to
proceed with intelligence. As he passed through
each curling mass the youth wondered what
would confront him on the farther side.

The command went painfully forward until an
open space interposed between them and the
lurid lines. Here, crouching and cowering behind
some trees, the men clung with desperation, as if
threatened by a wave. They looked wild-eyed,
and as if amazed at this furious disturbance they
had stirred. In the storm there was an ironical
expression of their importance. The faces of the
men, too, showed a lack of a certain feeling of
responsibility for being there. It was as if they
had been driven. It was the dominant animal failing to remember in the supreme moments the
forceful causes of various superficial qualities.
The whole affair seemed incomprehensible to
many of them.

As they halted thus the lieutenant again began
to bellow profanely. Regardless of the vindictive

threats of the bullets, he went about coaxing, berating, and bedamning. His lips, that were habitually in a soft and childlike curve, were now writhed into unholy contortions. He swore by all possible deities.

Once he grabbed the youth by the arm. "Come on, yeh lunkhead!" he roared. "Come on! We'll all git killed if we stay here. We've on'y got t' go across that lot. An' then"—the remainder of his idea disappeared in a blue haze of curses.

The youth stetched forth his arm. "Cross there?" His mouth was puckered in doubt and awe.

"Certainly. Jest 'cross th' lot! We can't stay here," screamed the lieutenant. He poked his face close to the youth and waved his bandaged hand. "Come on!" Presently he grappled with him as if for a wrestling bout. It was as if he planned to drag the youth by the ear on to the assault.

The private felt a sudden unspeakable indignation against his officer. He wrenched fiercely and shook him off.

"Come on yerself, then," he yelled. There was a bitter challenge in his voice.

They galloped together down the regimental

front. The friend scrambled after them. In front of the colors the three men began to bawl: "Come on! come on!" They danced and gyrated like tortured savages.

The flag, obedient to these appeals, bended its glittering form and swept toward them. The men wavered in indecision for a moment, and then with a long, wailful cry the dilapidated regiment surged forward and began its new journey.

Over the field went the scurrying mass. It was a handful of men splattered into the faces of the enemy. Toward it instantly sprang the yellow tongues. A vast quantity of blue smoke hung before them. A mighty banging made ears valueless.

The youth ran like a madman to reach the woods before a bullet could discover him. He ducked his head low, like a football player. In his haste his eyes almost closed, and the scene was a wild blur. Pulsating saliva stood at the corners of his mouth.

Within him, as he hurled himself forward, was born a love, a despairing fondness for this flag which was near him. It was a creation of beauty and invulnerability. It was a goddess, radiant, that bended its form with an imperious gesture to him. It was a woman, red and white, hating and loving, that called him with the voice of his hopes. Because no harm could come to it he endowed it with power. He kept near, as if it could be a saver of lives, and an imploring cry went from his mind.

In the mad scramble he was aware that the color sergeant flinched suddenly, as if struck by a bludgeon. He faltered, and then became motionless, save for his quivering knees.

He made a spring and a clutch at the pole. At the same instant his friend grabbed it from the other side. They jerked at it, stout and furious, but the color sergeant was dead, and the corpse would not relinquish its trust. For a moment there was a grim encounter. The dead man, swinging with bended back, seemed to be obstinately tugging, in ludicrous and awful ways, for the possession of the flag.

It was past in an instant of time. They wrenched the flag furiously from the dead man, and, as they turned again, the corpse swayed forward with bowed head. One arm swung high, and the curved hand fell with heavy protest on the friend's unheeding shoulder.

CHAPTER XX

WHEN the two youths turned with the flag they saw that much of the regiment had crumbled away, and the dejected remnant was coming back. The men, having hurled themselves in projectile fashion, had presently expended their forces. They slowly retreated, with their faces still toward the spluttering woods, and their hot rifles still replying to the din. Several officers were giving orders, their voices keyed to screams.

"Where in hell yeh goin'?" the lieutenant was asking in a sarcastic howl. And a red-bearded officer, whose voice of triple brass could plainly be heard, was commanding: "Shoot into 'em! Shoot into 'em, Gawd damn their souls!" There was a *mêlée* of screeches, in which the men were ordered to do conflicting and impossible things.

The youth and his friend had a small scuffle over the flag. "Give it t' me!" "No, let me keep it!" Each felt satisfied with the other's possession of it, but each felt bound to declare, by an offer to carry the emblem, his willingness to further risk himself. The youth roughly pushed his friend away.

The regiment fell back to the stolid trees. There it halted for a moment to blaze at some dark forms that had begun to steal upon its track. Presently it resumed its march again, curving among the tree trunks. By the time the depleted regiment had again reached the first open space they were receiving a fast and merciless fire. There seemed to be mobs all about them.

The greater part of the men, discouraged, their spirits worn by the turmoil, acted as if stunned. They accepted the pelting of the bullets with bowed and weary heads. It was of no purpose to strive against walls. It was of no use to batter themselves against granite. And from this consciousness that they had attempted to conquer an unconquerable thing there seemed to arise a feeling that they had been betrayed. They glowered with bent brows, but dangerously, upon some of the officers, more particularly upon the red-bearded one with the voice of triple brass.

However, the rear of the regiment was fringed

with men, who continued to shoot irritably at the advancing foes. They seemed resolved to make every trouble. The youthful lieutenant was perhaps the last man in the disordered mass. His forgotten back was toward the enemy. He had been shot in the arm. It hung straight and rigid. Occasionally he would cease to remember it, and be about to emphasize an oath with a sweeping gesture. The multiplied pain caused him to swear with incredible power.

The youth went along with slipping, uncertain feet. He kept watchful eyes rearward. A scowl of mortification and rage was upon his face. He had thought of a fine revenge upon the officer who had referred to him and his fellows as mule drivers. But he saw that it could not come to pass. His dreams had collapsed when the mule drivers, dwindling rapidly, had wavered and hesitated on the little clearing, and then had recoiled. And now the retreat of the mule drivers was a march of shame to him.

A dagger-pointed gaze from without his blackened face held toward the enemy, but his greater hatred was riveted upon the man, who, not knowing him, had called him a mule driver.

When he knew that he and his comrades had

failed to do anything in successful ways that might bring the little pangs of a kind of remorse upon the officer, the youth allowed the rage of the baffled to possess him. This cold officer upon a monument, who dropped epithets unconernedly down, would be finer as a dead man, he thought. So grievous did he think it that he could never possess the secret right to taunt truly in answer.

He had pictured red letters of curious revenge. "We *are* mule drivers, are we?" And now he was compelled to throw them away.

He presently wrapped his heart in the cloak of his pride and kept the flag erect. He harangued his fellows, pushing against their chests with his free hand. To those he knew well he made frantic appeals, beseeching them by name. Between him and the lieutenant, scolding and near to losing his mind with rage, there was felt a subtle fellowship and equality. They supported each other in all manner of hoarse, howling protests.

But the regiment was a machine run down. The two men babbled at a forceless thing. The soldiers who had heart to go slowly were continually shaken in their resolves by a knowledge that comrades were slipping with speed back to the lines. It was difficult to think of reputation when others were thinking of skins. Wounded men were left crying on this black journey.

The smoke fringes and flames blustered always. The youth, peering once through a sudden rift in a cloud, saw a brown mass of troops, interwoven and magnified until they appeared to be thousands. A fierce-hued flag flashed before his vision.

Immediately, as if the uplifting of the smoke had been prearranged, the discovered troops burst into a rasping yell, and a hundred flames jetted toward the retreating band. A rolling gray cloud again interposed as the regiment doggedly replied. The youth had to depend again upon his misused ears, which were trembling and buzzing from the *mêlée* of musketry and yells.

The way seemed eternal. In the clouded haze men became panic-stricken with the thought that the regiment had lost its path, and was proceeding in a perilous direction. Once the men who headed the wild procession turned and came pushing back against their comrades, screaming that they were being fired upon from points which they had considered to be toward their own lines. At this cry a hysterical fear and dismay beset the troops. A soldier, who heretofore had been ambitious to make the regiment into a wise little band that would proceed calmly amid the huge-appearing difficulties, suddenly sank down and buried his face in his arms with an air of bowing to a doom. From another a shrill lamentation rang out filled with profane allusions to a general. Men ran hither and thither, seeking with their eyes roads of escape.

With serene regularity, as if controlled by a schedule, bullets buffed into men.

The youth walked stolidly into the midst of the mob, and with his flag in his hands took a stand as if he expected an attempt to push him to the ground. He unconsciously assumed the attitude of the color bearer in the fight of the preceding day. He passed over his brow a hand that trembled. His breath did not come freely. He was choking during this small wait for the crisis.

His friend came to him. "Well, Henry, I guess this is good-by-John."

"Oh, shut up, you damned fool!" replied the youth, and he would not look at the other.

The officers labored like politicians to beat the mass into a proper circle to face the menaces. The ground was uneven and torn. The men curled into depressions and fitted themselves snugly behind whatever would frustrate a bullet.

The youth noted with vague surprise that the lieutenant was standing mutely with his legs far apart and his sword held in the manner of a cane. The youth wondered what had happened to his vocal organs that he no more cursed.

There was something curious in this little intent pause of the lieutenant. He was like a babe which, having wept its fill, raises its eyes and fixes them upon a distant toy. He was engrossed in this contemplation, and the soft under lip quivered from self-whispered words.

Some lazy and ignorant smoke curled slowly. The men, hiding from the bullets, waited anxiously for it to lift and disclose the plight of the regiment.

The silent ranks were suddenly thrilled by the eager voice of the youthful lieutenant bawling out: "Here they come! Right on to us, b'Gawd!" His further words were lost in a roar of wicked thunder from the men's rifles.

The youth's eyes had instantly turned in the direction indicated by the awakened and agitated lieutenant, and he had seen the haze of treachery disclosing a body of soldiers of the enemy. They were so near that he could see their features. There was a recognition as he looked at the types of faces. Also he perceived with dim amazement that their uniforms were rather gay in effect, being light gray, accented with a brilliant-hued facing. Moreover, the clothes seemed new.

These troops had apparently been going forward with caution, their rifles held in readiness, when the youthful lieutenant had discovered them and their movement had been interrupted by the volley from the blue regiment. From the moment's glimpse, it was derived that they had been unaware of the proximity of their dark-suited foes or had mistaken the direction. Almost instantly they were shut utterly from the youth's sight by the smoke from the energetic rifles of his companions. He strained his vision to learn the accomplishment of the volley, but the smoke hung before him.

The two bodies of troops exchanged blows in the manner of a pair of boxers. The fast angry firings went back and forth. The men in blue were intent with the despair of their circumstances and they seized upon the revenge to be had at close range. Their thunder swelled loud and valiant. Their curving front bristled with flashes and the place resounded with the clangor of their ramrods. The youth ducked and dodged for a time and achieved a few unsatisfactory views of the enemy. There appeared to be many of them and they were replying swiftly. They seemed moving toward the blue regiment, step by step. He seated himself gloomily on the ground with his flag between his knees.

As he noted the vicious, wolflike temper of his comrades he had a sweet thought that if the enemy was about to swallow the regimental broom as a large prisoner, it could at least have the consolation of going down with bristles forward.

But the blows of the antagonist began to grow more weak. Fewer bullets ripped the air, and finally, when the men slackened to learn of the fight, they could see only dark, floating smoke. The regiment lay still and gazed. Presently some chance whim came to the pestering blur, and it began to coil heavily away. The men saw a ground vacant of fighters. It would have been an empty stage if it were not for a few corpses that lay thrown and twisted into fantastic shapes upon the sward.

At sight of this tableau, many of the men in

blue sprang from behind their covers and made
an ungainly dance of joy. Their eyes burned and
a hoarse cheer of elation broke from their dry
lips.

It had begun to seem to them that events were
trying to prove that they were impotent. These
little battles had evidently endeavored to demonstrate that the men could not fight well. When on
the verge of submission to these opinions, the
small duel had showed them that the proportions
were not impossible, and by it they had revenged
themselves upon their misgivings and upon the
foe.

The impetus of enthusiasm was theirs again.
They gazed about them with looks of uplifted
pride, feeling new trust in the grim, always confident weapons in their hands. And they were
men.

CHAPTER XXI

PRESENTLY they knew that no fighting threatened them. All ways seemed once more opened to them. The dusty blue lines of their friends were disclosed a short distance away. In the distance there were many colossal noises, but in all this part of the field there was a sudden stillness.

They perceived that they were free. The depleted band drew a long breath of relief and gathered itself into a bunch to complete its trip.

In this last length of journey the men began to show strange emotions. They hurried with nervous fear. Some who had been dark and unfaltering in the grimmest moments now could not conceal an anxiety that made them frantic. It was perhaps that they dreaded to be killed in insignificant ways after the times for proper military deaths had passed. Or, perhaps, they thought it would be too ironical to get killed at the portals of safety. With backward looks of perturbation, they hastened.

As they approached their own lines there was some sarcasm exhibited on the part of a gaunt and bronzed regiment that lay resting in the shade of trees. Questions were wafted to them.

"Where th' hell yeh been?"

"What yeh comin' back fer?"

"Why didn't yeh stay there?"

"Was it warm out there, sonny?"

"Goin' home now, boys?"

One shouted in taunting mimicry: "Oh, mother, come quick an' look at th' sojers!"

There was no reply from the bruised and battered regiment, save that one man made broadcast challenges to fist fights and the red-bearded officer walked rather near and glared in great swashbuckler style at a tall captain in the other regiment. But the lieutenant suppressed the man who wished to fist fight, and the tall captain, flushing at the little fanfare of the red-bearded one, was obliged to look intently at some trees.

The youth's tender flesh was deeply stung by these remarks. From under his creased brows he glowered with hate at the mockers. He meditated upon a few revenges. Still, many in the regiment hung their heads in criminal fashion, so that it came to pass that the men trudged with sudden heaviness, as if they bore upon their bended shoulders the coffln of their honor. And the youthful lieutenant, recollecting himself, began to mutter softly in black curses.

They turned when they arrived at their old position to regard the ground over which they had charged.

The youth in this contemplation was smitten with a large astonishment. He discovered that the distances, as compared with the brilliant measurings of his mind, were trivial and ridiculous. The stolid trees, where much had taken place, seemed incredibly near. The time, too, now that he reflected, he saw to have been short. He wondered at the number of emotions and events that had been crowded into such little spaces. Elfin thoughts must have exaggerated and enlarged everything, he said.

It seemed, then, that there was bitter justice in the speeches of the gaunt and bronzed veterans. He veiled a glance of disdain at his fellows who strewed the ground, choking with dust, red from perspiration, misty-eyed, disheveled.

They were gulping at their canteens, fierce to wring every mite of water from them, and they polished at their swollen and watery features with coat sleeves and bunches of grass.

However, to the youth there was a considerable joy in musing upon his performances during the charge. He had had very little time previously in which to appreciate himself, so that there was now much satisfaction in quietly thinking of his actions. He recalled bits of color that in the flurry had stamped themselves unawares upon his engaged senses.

As the regiment lay heaving from its hot exertions the officer who had named them as mule drivers came galloping along the line. He had lost his cap. His tousled hair streamed wildly, and his face was dark with vexation and wrath. His temper was displayed with more clearness by the way in which he managed his horse. He jerked and wrenched savagely at his bridle, stopping the hard-breathing animal with a furious pull near the colonel of the regiment. He immediately exploded in reproaches which came unbidden to the ears of the men. They were suddenly alert, being always curious about black words between officers.

"Oh, thunder, MacChesnay, what an awful bull you made of this thing!" began the officer. He attempted low tones, but his indignation caused certain of the men to learn the sense of his words. "What an awful mess you made! Good Lord, man, you stopped about a hundred feet this side of a very pretty success! If your men had gone a hundred feet farther you would have made a great charge, but as it is—what a lot of mud diggers you've got anyway!"

The men, listening with bated breath, now turned their curious eyes upon the colonel. They had a ragamuffin interest in this affair.

The colonel was seen to straighten his form and put one hand forth in oratorical fashion. He wore an injured air; it was as if a deacon had been accused of stealing. The men were wiggling in an ecstasy of excitement.

But of a sudden the colonel's manner changed from that of a deacon to that of a Frenchman. He shrugged his shoulders. "Oh, well, general, we went as far as we could," he said calmly.

"As far as you could? Did you, b'Gawd?" snorted the other. "Well, that wasn't very far, was it?" he added, with a glance of cold contempt into the other's eyes. "Not very far, I think. You were intended to make a diversion in favor of Whiterside. How well you succeeded your own ears can now tell you." He wheeled his horse and rode stiffly away.

The colonel, bidden to hear the jarring noises of an engagement in the woods to the left, broke out in vague damnations.

The lieutenant, who had listened with an air of impotent rage to the interview, spoke suddenly in firm and undaunted tones. "I don't care what a man is—whether he is a general or what—if he says th' boys didn't put up a good fight out there he's a damned fool."

"Lieutenant," began the colonel, severely, "this is my own affair, and I'll trouble you . . ."

The lieutenant made an obedient gesture. "All right, colonel, all right," he said. He sat down with an air of being content with himself.

The news that the regiment had been reproached went along the line. For a time the men were bewildered by it. "Good thunder!" they ejaculated, staring at the vanishing form of the general. They conceived it to be a huge mistake.

Presently, however, they began to believe that in truth their efforts had been called light. The youth could see this conviction weigh upon the entire regiment until the men were like cuffed and cursed animals, but withal rebellious.

The friend, with a grievance in his eye, went to the youth. "I wonder what he does want," he said. "He must think we went out there an' played marbles! I never see sech a man!"

The youth developed a tranquil philosophy for these moments of irritation. "Oh, well," he rejoined, "he probably didn't see nothing of it at all and got mad as blazes, and concluded we were a lot of sheep, just because we didn't do what he wanted done. It's a pity old Grandpa Henderson got killed yesterday—he'd have known that we did our best and fought good. It's just our awful luck, that's what."

"I should say so," replied the friend. He seemed to be deeply wounded at an injustice. "I should say we did have awful luck! There's no fun in fightin' fer people when everything yeh do—no matter what—ain't done right. I have a notion t' stay behind next time an' let 'em take their ol' charge an' go t' th' devil with it."

The youth spoke soothingly to his comrade. "Well, we both did good. I'd like to see the fool what'd say we both didn't do as good as we could!"

"Of course we did," declared the friend stoutly. "An' I'd break th' feller's neck if he was as big as a church. But we're all right, anyhow, for I heard one feller say that we two fit th' best in th' reg'ment, an' they had a great argument 'bout it. Another feller, 'a course, he had t' up an' say it was a lie—he seen all what was goin' on an' he never seen us from th' beginnin' t' th' end. An' a lot more struck in an' ses it wasn't a lie— we did fight like thunder, an' they give us quite a send-off. But this is what I can't stand—these everlastin' ol' soldiers, titterin' an' laughin', an' then that general, he's crazy."

The youth exclaimed with sudden exaspera- tion: "He's a lunkhead! He makes me mad. I wish he'd come along next time. We'd show 'im what—"

He ceased because several men had come hur- rying up. Their faces expressed a bringing of great news.

"O Flem, yeh jest oughta heard!" cried one, eagerly.

"Heard what?" said the youth.

"Yeh jest oughta heard!" repeated the other, and he arranged himself to tell his tidings. The others made an excited circle. "Well, sir, th' colonel met your lieutenant right by us—it was damnedest thing I ever heard—an' he ses: 'Ahem! ahem!' he ses. 'Mr. Hasbrouck!' he ses, 'by th' way, who was that lad what carried th' flag?' he ses. There, Flemin', what d' yeh think 'a that? 'Who was th' lad what carried th' flag?' he ses, an' th' lieutenant, he speaks up right away: 'That's Flemin', an' he's a jimhickey,' he ses, right away. What? I say he did. 'A jimhickey,' he ses—those 'r his words. He did, too. I say he did. If you kin tell this story better than I kin, go ahead an' tell it. Well, then, keep yer mouth shet. Th' lieutenant, he ses: 'He's a jimhickey,' an' th' colonel, he ses: 'Ahem! ahem! he is, indeed, a very good man t' have, ahem! He kep' th' flag 'way t' th' front. I saw 'im. He's a good un,' ses th' colonel. 'You bet,' ses th' lieutenant, 'he an' a feller named Wilson was at th' head 'f th' charge, an' howlin' like Indians all th' time,' he ses. 'A feller named Wilson,' he ses. There, Wilson, m'boy, put that in a letter an' send it hum t' yer mother, hay? 'A feller named Wilson,' he ses. An' th' colonel, he ses: 'Were they, indeed? Ahem! ahem! My sakes!' he ses. 'At th' head a' th' reg'ment?' he ses. 'They were,' ses th' lieutenant. 'My sakes!' ses th' colonel. He ses: 'Well,

well, well,' he ses, 'those two babies?' 'They were,' ses th' lieutenant. 'Well, well,' ses th' colonel, 'they deserve t' be major-generals,' he ses. 'They deserve t' be major-generals.' "

The youth and his friend had said: "Huh!" "Yer lyin', Thompson." "Oh, go t' blazes!" "He never sed it." "Oh, what a lie!" "Huh!" But despite these youthful scoffings and embarrassments, they knew that their faces were deeply flushing from thrills of pleasure. They exchanged a secret glance of joy and congratulation.

They speedily forgot many things. The past held no pictures of error and disappointment. They were very happy, and their hearts swelled with grateful affection for the colonel and the youthful lieutenant.

CHAPTER XXII

WHEN the woods again began to pour forth the dark-hued masses of the enemy the youth felt serene self-confidence. He smiled briefly when he saw men dodge and duck at the long screechings of shells that were thrown in giant handfuls over them. He stood, erect and tranquil, watching the attack begin against a part of the line that made a blue curve along the side of an adjacent hill. His vision being unmolested by smoke from the rifles of his companions, he had opportunities to see parts of the hard fight. It was a relief to perceive at last from whence came some of these noises which had been roared into his ears.

Off a short way he saw two regiments fighting a little separate battle with two other regiments. It was in a cleared space, wearing a set-apart look. They were blazing as if upon a wager, giving and taking tremendous blows. The firings were incredibly fierce and rapid. These intent regiments apparently were oblivious of all larger purposes of war, and were slugging each other as if at a matched game.

In another direction he saw a magnificent brigade going with the evident intention of driving the enemy from a wood. They passed in out of sight and presently there was a most awe-inspiring racket in the wood. The noise was unspeakable. Having stirred this prodigious uproar, and, apparently, finding it too prodigious, the brigade, after a little time, came marching airily out again with its fine formation in nowise disturbed. There were no traces of speed in its movements. The brigade was jaunty and seemed to point a proud thumb at the yelling wood.

On a slope to the left there was a long row of guns, gruff and maddened, denouncing the enemy, who, down through the woods, were forming for another attack in the pitiless monotony of conflicts. The round red discharges from the guns made a crimson flare and a high, thick smoke. Occasional glimpses could be caught of groups of the toiling artillerymen. In the rear of this row of guns stood a house, calm and white, amid bursting shells. A congregation of horses, tied to a long railing, were tugging frenziedly at their bridles. Men were running hither and thither.

The detached battle between the four regiments lasted for some time. There chanced to be no interference, and they settled their dispute by themselves. They struck savagely and powerfully at each other for a period of minutes, and then the lighter-hued regiments faltered and drew back, leaving the dark-blue lines shouting. The youth could see the two flags shaking with laughter amid the smoke remnants.

Presently there was a stillness, pregnant with meaning. The blue lines shifted and changed a trifle and stared expectantly at the silent woods and fields before them. The hush was solemn and churchlike, save for a distant battery that, evidently unable to remain quiet, sent a faint rolling thunder over the ground. It irritated, like the noises of unimpressed boys. The men imagined that it would prevent their perched ears from hearing the first words of the new battle.

Of a sudden the guns on the slope roared out a message of warning. A spluttering sound had begun in the woods. It swelled with amazing speed to a profound clamor that involved the earth in noises. The splitting crashes swept along the lines until an interminable roar was developed. To those in the midst of it it became a din fitted to the universe. It was the whirring and thumping of gigantic machinery, complications among the smaller stars. The youth's ears were filled cups. They were incapable of hearing more.

On an incline over which a road wound he saw wild and desperate rushes of men perpetually backward and forward in riotous surges. These parts of the opposing armies were two long waves that pitched upon each other madly at dictated points. To and fro they swelled. Sometimes, one side by its yells and cheers would proclaim decisive blows, but a moment later the other side would be all yells and cheers. Once the youth saw a spray of light forms go in houndlike leaps toward the waving blue lines. There was much howling, and presently it went away with a vast mouthful of prisoners. Again, he saw a blue wave dash with such thunderous force against a gray obstruction that it seemed to clear the earth of it and leave nothing but trampled sod. And always in their swift and deadly rushes to and fro the men screamed and yelled like maniacs.

Particular pieces of fence or secure positions behind collections of trees were wrangled over, as gold thrones or pearl bedsteads. There were desperate lunges at these chosen spots seemingly every instant, and most of them were bandied like light toys between the contending forces. The youth could not tell from the battle flags flying like crimson foam in many directions which color of cloth was winning.

His emaciated regiment bustled forth with undiminished fierceness when its time came. When assaulted again by bullets, the men burst out in a barbaric cry of rage and pain. They bent their heads in aims of intent hatred behind the projected hammers of their guns. Their ramrods clanged loud with fury as their eager arms pounded the cartridges into the rifle barrels. The front of the regiment was a smoke-wall penetrated by the flashing points of yellow and red.

Wallowing in the fight, they were in an astonishingly short time resmudged. They surpassed in stain and dirt all their previous appearances. Moving to and fro with strained exertion, jabbering the while, they were, with their swaying bodies, black faces, and glowing eyes, like strange and ugly fiends jigging heavily in the smoke.

The lieutenant, returning from a tour after a bandage, produced from a hidden receptacle of his mind new and portentous oaths suited to the emergency. Strings of expletives he swung lash-like over the backs of his men, and it was evident that his previous efforts had in nowise impaired his resources.

The youth, still the bearer of the colors, did not feel his idleness. He was deeply absorbed as a spectator. The crash and swing of the great drama made him lean forward, intent-eyed, his face working in small contortions. Sometimes he prattled, words coming unconsciously from him in grotesque exclamations. He did not know that he breathed; that the flag hung silently over him, so absorbed was he.

A formidable line of the enemy came within dangerous range. They could be seen plainly— tall, gaunt men with excited faces running with long strides toward a wandering fence.

At sight of this danger the men suddenly ceased their cursing monotone. There was an instant of strained silence before they threw up their rifles and fired a plumping volley at the foes. There had been no order given; the men, upon recognizing the menace, had immediately let drive their flock of bullets without waiting for word of command.

But the enemy were quick to gain the protection of the wandering line of fence. They slid down behind it with remarkable celerity, and from this position they began briskly to slice up the blue men.

The latter braced their energies for a great struggle. Often, white clinched teeth shone from the dusky faces. Many heads surged to and fro, floating upon a pale sea of smoke. Those behind the fence frequently shouted and yelped in taunts and gibelike cries, but the regiment maintained a stressed silence. Perhaps, at this new assault the men recalled the fact that they had been named mud diggers, and it made their situation thrice bitter. They were breathlessly intent upon keeping the ground and thrusting away the rejoicing body of the enemy. They fought swiftly and with a despairing savageness denoted in their expressions.

The youth had resolved not to budge whatever should happen. Some arrows of scorn that had buried themselves in his heart had generated strange and unspeakable hatred. It was clear to him that his final and absolute revenge was to be

achieved by his dead body lying, torn and glut-
tering, upon the field. This was to be a poignant
retaliation upon the officer who had said "mule
drivers," and later "mud diggers," for in all the
wild graspings of his mind for a unit responsible
for his sufferings and commotions he always
seized upon the man who had dubbed him
wrongly. And it was his idea, vaguely formulated,
that his corpse would be for those eyes a great
and salt reproach.

The regiment bled extravagantly. Grunting
bundles of blue began to drop. The orderly
sergeant of the youth's company was shot through
the cheeks. Its supports being injured, his jaw
hung afar down, disclosing in the wide cavern of
his mouth a pulsing mass of blood and teeth.
And with it all he made attempts to cry out. In
his endeavor there was a dreadful earnestness, as
if he conceived that one great shriek would make
him well.

The youth saw him presently go rearward. His
strength seemed in nowise impaired. He ran
swiftly, casting wild glances for succor.

Others fell down about the feet of their companions. Some of the wounded crawled out and

away, but many lay still, their bodies twisted into impossible shapes.

The youth looked once for his friend. He saw a vehement young man, powder-smeared and frowzled, whom he knew to be him. The lieutenant, also, was unscathed in his position at the rear. He had continued to curse, but it was now with the air of a man who was using his last box of oaths.

For the fire of the regiment had begun to wane and drip. The robust voice, that had come strangely from the thin ranks, was growing rapidly weak.

CHAPTER XXIII

THE colonel came running along back of the line. There were other officers following him. "We must charge'm!" they shouted. "We must charge'm!" they cried with resentful voices, as if anticipating a rebellion against this plan by the men.

The youth, upon hearing the shouts, began to study the distance between him and the enemy. He made vague calculations. He saw that to be firm soldiers they must go forward. It would be death to stay in the present place, and with all the circumstances to go backward would exalt too many others. Their hope was to push the galling foes away from the fence.

He expected that his companions, weary and stiffened, would have to be driven to this assault, but as he turned toward them he perceived with a certain surprise that they were giving quick and unqualified expressions of assent. There was an ominous, clanging overture to the charge when the shafts of the bayonets rattled upon the rifle barrels. At the yelled words of command the soldiers sprang forward in eager leaps. There was new and unexpected force in the movement of the regiment. A knowledge of its faded and jaded condition made the charge appear like a paroxysm, a display of the strength that comes before a final feebleness. The men scampered in insane fever of haste, racing as if to achieve a sudden success before an exhilarating fluid should leave them. It was a blind and despairing rush by the collection of men in dusty and tattered blue, over a green sward and under a sapphire sky, toward a fence, dimly outlined in smoke, from behind which spluttered the fierce rifles of enemies.

The youth kept the bright colors to the front. He was waving his free arm in furious circles, the while shrieking mad calls and appeals, urging on those that did not need to be urged, for it seemed that the mob of blue men hurling themselves on the dangerous group of rifles were again grown suddenly wild with an enthusiasm of unselfishness. From the many firings starting toward them, it looked as if they would merely succeed in making a great sprinkling of corpses on the grass between their former position and the fence. But they were in a state of frenzy, perhaps becaue of forgotten vanities, and it made an exhibition of sublime recklessness. There was no obvious questioning, nor figurings, nor diagrams. There were, apparently, no considered loopholes. It appeared that the swift wings of their desires would have shattered against the iron gates of the impossible.

He himself felt the daring spirit of a savage, religion-mad. He was capable of profound sacrifices, a tremendous death. He had no time for dissections, but he knew that he thought of the bullets only as things that could prevent him from reaching the place of his endeavor. There were subtle flashings of joy within him that thus should be his mind.

He strained all his strength. His eyesight was shaken and dazzled by the tension of thought and muscle. He did not see anything excepting the mist of smoke gashed by the little knives of fire, but he knew that in it lay the aged fence of a vanished farmer protecting the snuggled bodies of the gray men.

As he ran a thought of the shock of contact

gleamed in his mind. He expected a great con-
cussion when the two bodies of troops crashed
together. This became a part of his wild battle
madness. He could feel the onward swing of the
regiment about him and he conceived of a thunderous, crushing blow that would prostrate the
resistance and spread consternation and amazement for miles. The flying regiment was going to
have a catapultian effect. This dream made him
run faster among his comrades, who were giving
vent to hoarse and frantic cheers.

But presently he could see that many of the
men in gray did not intend to abide the blow. The
smoke, rolling, disclosed men who ran, their faces
still turned. These grew to a crowd, who retired
stubbornly. Individuals wheeled frequently to
send a bullet at the blue wave.

But at one part of the line there was a grim and
obdurate group that made no movement. They
were settled firmly down behind posts and rails.
A flag, ruffled and fierce, waved over them and
their rifles dinned fiercely.

The blue whirl of men got very near, until it
seemed that in truth there would be a close and
frightful scuffle. There was an expressed disdain
in the opposition of the little group, that changed

the meaning of the cheers of the men in blue. They became yells of wrath, directed, personal. The cries of the two parties were now in sound an interchange of scathing insults.

They in blue showed their teeth; their eyes shone all white. They launched themselves as at the throats of those who stood resisting. The space between dwindled to an insignificant distance.

The youth had centered the gaze of his soul upon that other flag. Its possession would be high pride. It would express bloody minglings, near blows. He had a gigantic hatred for those who made great difficulties and complications. They caused it to be as a craved treasure of mythology, hung amid tasks and contrivances of danger.

He plunged like a mad horse at it. He was resolved it should not escape if wild blows and darings of blows could seize it. His own emblem, quivering and aflare, was winging toward the other. It seemed there would shortly be an encounter of strange beaks and claws, as of eagles.

The swirling body of blue men came to a sudden halt at close and disastrous range and roared a swift volley. The group in gray was split and broken by this fire, but its riddled body still fought. The men in blue yelled again and rushed in upon it.

The youth, in his leapings, saw, as through a mist, a picture of four or five men stretched upon the ground or writhing upon their knees with bowed heads as if they had been stricken by bolts from the sky. Tottering among them was the rival color bearer, whom the youth saw had been bitten vitally by the bullets of the last formidable volley. He perceived this man fighting a last struggle, the struggle of one whose legs are grasped by demons. It was a ghastly battle. Over his face was the bleach of death, but set upon it were the dark and hard lines of desperate purpose. With this terrible grin of resolution he hugged his precious flag to him and was stumbling and staggering in his design to go the way that led to safety for it.

But his wounds always made it seem that his feet were retarded, held, and he fought a grim fight, as with invisible ghouls fastened greedily upon his limbs. Those in advance of the scampering blue men, howling cheers, leaped at the fence. The despair of the lost was in his eyes as he glanced back at them.

The youth's friend went over the obstruction in a tumbling heap and sprang at the flag as a panther at prey. He pulled at it and, wrenching it free, swung up its red brilliancy with a mad cry of exultation even as the color bearer, gasping, lurched over in a final throe and, stiffening convulsively, turned his dead face to the ground. There was much blood upon the grass blades.

At the place of success there began more wild clamorings of cheers. The men gesticulated and bellowed in an ecstasy. When they spoke it was as if they considered their listener to be a mile away. What hats and caps were left to them they often slung high in the air.

At one part of the line four men had been swooped upon, and they now sat as prisoners. Some blue men were about them in an eager and curious circle. The soldiers had trapped strange birds, and there was an examination. A flurry of fast questions was in the air.

One of the prisoners was nursing a superficial wound in the foot. He cuddled it, babywise, but he looked up from it often to curse with an astonishing utter abandon straight at the noses of his captors. He consigned them to red regions; he called upon the pestilential wrath of strange gods.

And with it all he was singularly free from recognition of the finer points of the conduct of prisoners of war. It was as if a clumsy clod had trod upon his toe and he conceived it to be his privilege, his duty, to use deep, resentful oaths.

Another, who was a boy in years, took his plight with great calmness and apparent good nature. He conversed with the men in blue, studying their faces with his bright and keen eyes. They spoke of battles and conditions. There was an acute interest in all their faces during this exchange of viewpoints. It seemed a great satisfaction to hear voices from where all had been darkness and speculation.

The third captive sat with a morose countenance. He preserved a stoical and cold attitude. To all advances he made one reply without variation, "Ah, go t' hell!"

The last of the four was always silent and, for the most part, kept his face turned in unmolested directions. From the views the youth received he seemed to be in a state of absolute dejection. Shame was upon him, and with it profound regret that he was, perhaps, no more to be counted in the ranks of his fellows. The youth could detect no expression that would allow him to believe that the other was giving a thought to his narrowed future, the pictured dungeons, perhaps, and starvations and brutalities, liable to the imagination. All to be seen was shame for captivity and regret for the right to antagonize.

After the men had celebrated sufficiently they settled down behind the old rail fence, on the opposite side to the one from which their foes had been driven. A few shot perfunctorily at distant marks.

There was some long grass. The youth nestled in it and rested, making a convenient rail support the flag. His friend, jubilant and glorified, holding his treasure with vanity, came to him there. They sat side by side and congratulated each other.

CHAPTER XXIV

THE roarings that had stretched in a long line of sound across the face of the forest began to grow intermittent and weaker. The stentorian speeches of the artillery continued in some distant encounter, but the crashes of the musketry had almost ceased. The youth and his friend of a sudden looked up, feeling a deadened form of distress at the waning of these noises, which had become a part of life. They could see changes going on among the troops. There were marchings this way and that way. A battery wheeled leisurely. On the crest of a small hill was the thick gleam of many departing muskets.

The youth arose. "Well, what now, I wonder?" he said. By his tone he seemed to be preparing to resent some new monstrosity in the way of dins and smashes. He shaded his eyes with his grimy hand and gazed over the field.

His friend also arose and stared. "I bet we're goin' t' git along out of this an' back over th' river," said he.

"Well, I swan!" said the youth.

They waited, watching. Within a little while the regiment received orders to retrace its way. The men got up grunting from the grass, regretting the soft repose. They jerked their stiffened legs, and stretched their arms over their heads. One man swore as he rubbed his eyes. They all groaned "O Lord!" They had as many objections to this change as they would have had to a proposal for a new battle.

They trampled slowly back over the field across which they had run in a mad scamper.

The regiment marched until it had joined its fellows. The re-formed brigade, in column, aimed through a wood at the road. Directly they were in a mass of dust-covered troops, and were trudging along in a way parallel to the enemy's lines as these had been defined by the previous turmoil.

They passed within view of a stolid white house, and saw in front of it groups of their comrades lying in wait behind a neat breastwork. A row of guns were booming at a distant enemy.

Shells thrown in reply were raising clouds of dust and splinters. Horsemen dashed along the line of intrenchments.

At this point of its march the division curved away from the field and went winding off in the direction of the river. When the significance of this movement had impressed itself upon the youth he turned his head and looked over his shoulder toward the trampled and *débris*-strewed ground. He breathed a breath of new satisfaction. He finally nudged his friend. "Well, it's all over," he said to him.

His friend gazed backward. "B'Gawd, it is," he assented. They mused.

For a time the youth was obliged to reflect in a puzzled and uncertain way. His mind was undergoing a subtle change. It took moments for it to cast off its battleful ways and resume its accustomed course of thought. Gradually his brain emerged from the clogged clouds, and at last he was enabled to more closely comprehend himself and circumstance.

He understood then that the existence of shot and counter-shot was in the past. He had dwelt in a land of strange, squalling upheavals and had come forth. He had been where there was red of blood and black of passion, and he was escaped. His first thoughts were given to rejoicings at this fact.

Later he began to study his deeds, his failures, and his achievements. Thus, fresh from scenes where many of his usual machines of reflection had been idle, from where he had proceeded sheeplike, he struggled to marshal all his acts.

At last they marched before him clearly. From this present viewpoint he was enabled to look upon them in spectator fashion and to criticize them with some correctness, for his new condition had already defeated certain sympathies.

Regarding his procession of memory he felt gleeful and unregretting, for in it his public deeds were paraded in great and shining prominence. Those performances which had been witnessed by his fellows marched now in wide purple and gold, having various deflections. They went gayly with music. It was pleasure to watch these things. He spent delightful minutes viewing the gilded images of memory.

He saw that he was good. He recalled with a thrill of joy the respectful comments of his fellows upon his conduct.

Nevertheless, the ghost of his flight from the

first engagement appeared to him and danced. There were small shoutings in his brain about these matters. For a moment he blushed, and the light of his soul flickered with shame.

A specter of reproach came to him. There loomed the dogging memory of the tattered soldier—he who, gored by bullets and faint for blood, had fretted concerning an imagined wound in another; he who had loaned his last of strength and intellect for the tall soldier; he who, blind with weariness and pain, had been deserted in the field.

For an instant a wretched chill of sweat was upon him at the thought that he might be detected in the thing. As he stood persistently before his vision, he gave vent to a cry of sharp irritation and agony.

His friend turned. "What's the matter, Henry?" he demanded. The youth's reply was an outburst of crimson oaths.

As he marched along the little branch-hung roadway among his prattling companions this vision of cruelty brooded over him. It clung near him always and darkened his view of these deeds in purple and gold. Whichever way his thoughts turned they were followed by the somber phantom of the desertion in the fields. He looked stealthily at his companions, feeling sure that they must discern in his face evidences of this pursuit. But they were plodding in ragged array, discussing with quick tongues the accomplishments of the late battle.

"Oh, if a man should come up an' ask me, I'd say we got a dum good lickin'."

"Lickin'—in yer eye! We ain't licked, sonny. We're going down here aways, swing aroun', an' come in behint 'em."

"Oh, hush, with your comin' in behint 'em. I've seen all 'a that I wanta. Don't tell me about comin' in behint . . ."

"Bill Smithers, he ses he'd rather been in ten hundred battles than been in that heluva hospital. He ses they got shootin' in th' nighttime, an' shells dropped plum among 'em in th' hospital. He ses sech hollerin' he never see."

"Hasbrouck? He's th' best off'cer in this here reg'ment. He's a whale."

"Didn't I tell yeh we'd come aroun' in behint 'em? Didn't I tell yeh so? We . . ."

"Oh, shet yer mouth!"

For a time this pursuing recollection of the tattered man took all elation from the youth's veins.

He saw his vivid error, and he was afraid that it would stand before him all his life. He took no share in the chatter of his comrades, nor did he look at them or know them, save when he felt sudden suspicion that they were seeing his thoughts and scrutinizing each detail of the scene with the tattered soldier.

Yet gradually he mustered force to put the sin at a distance. And at last his eyes seemed to open to some new ways. He found that he could look back upon the brass and bombast of his earlier gospels and see them truly. He was gleeful when he discovered that he now despised them.

With the conviction came a store of assurance. He felt a quiet manhood, non-assertive but of sturdy and strong blood. He knew that he would no more quail before his guides wherever they should point. He had been to touch the great death, and found that, after all, it was but the great death. He was a man.

So it came to pass that as he trudged from the place of blood and wrath his soul changed. He came from hot plowshares to prospects of clover tranquilly, and it was as if hot plowshares were not. Scars faded as flowers.

It rained. The procession of weary soldiers

became a bedraggled train, despondent and muttering, marching with churning effort in a trough of liquid brown mud under a low, wretched sky. Yet the youth smiled, for he saw that the world was a world for him, though many discovered it to be made of oaths and walking sticks. He had rid himself of the red sickness of battle. The sultry nightmare was in the past. He had been an animal blistered and sweating in the heat and pain of war. He turned now with a lover's thirst to images of tranquil skies, fresh meadows, cool brooks—an existence of soft and eternal peace.

Over the river a golden ray of sun came through the hosts of leaden rain clouds.

THE
VETERAN

OUT of the low window could be seen three hickory trees placed irregularly in a meadow that was resplendent in springtime green. Farther away, the old, dismal belfry of the village church loomed over the pines. A horse meditating in the shade of one of the hickories lazily swished his tail. The warm sunshine made an oblong of vivid yellow on the floor of the grocery.

"Could you see the whites of their eyes?" said the man who was seated on a soap box.

"Nothing of the kind," replied old Henry warmly. "Just a lot of flitting figures, and I let go at where they 'peared to be the thickest. Bang!"

"Mr. Fleming," said the grocer—his deferential voice expressed somehow the old man's exact social weight—"Mr. Fleming, you never was frightened much in them battles, was you?"

The veteran looked down and grinned. Observing his manner, the entire group tittered. "Well, I guess I was," he answered finally. "Pretty well scared, sometimes. Why, in my first battle I thought the sky was falling down. I thought the world was coming to an end. You bet I was scared."

Every one laughed. Perhaps it seemed strange and rather wonderful to them that a man should admit the thing, and in the tone of their laughter there was probably more admiration than if old Fleming had declared that he had always been a lion. Moreover, they knew that he had ranked as an orderly sergeant, and so their opinion of his heroism was fixed. None, to be sure, knew how an orderly sergeant ranked, but then it was understood to be somewhere just shy of a major general's stars. So, when old Henry admitted that he had been frightened, there was a laugh.

"The trouble was," said the old man, "I thought they were all shooting at me. Yes, sir, I thought every man in the other army was aiming at me in particular, and only me. And it seemed so darned unreasonable, you know. I wanted to explain to 'em what an almighty good fellow I was, because I thought then they might quit all trying to hit me. But I couldn't explain, and they kept on being unreasonable—blim!—blam!—bang! So I run!"

Two little triangles of wrinkles appeared at the corners of his eyes. Evidently he appreciated some comedy in this recital. Down near his feet, however, little Jim, his grandson, was visibly horror-stricken. His hands were clasped nervously, and his eyes were wide with astonishment at this terrible scandal, his most magnificent grandfather telling such a thing.

"That was at Chancellorsville. Of course, afterward I got kind of used to it. A man does. Lots of men, though, seem to feel all right from the start. I did, as soon as I 'got on to it,' as they say now; but at first I was pretty well flustered. Now, there was young Jim Conklin, old Si Conklin's son—that used to keep the tannery—you none of you recollect him—well, he went into it from the start just as if he was born to it. But with me it was different. I had to get used to it."

When little Jim walked with his grandfather he was in the habit of skipping along on the stone pavement in front of the three stores and the hotel of the town and betting that he could avoid the cracks. But upon this day he walked soberly, with his hand gripping two of his grandfather's fingers. Sometimes he kicked abstractedly at dandelions that curved over the walk. Any one could see that he was much troubled.

"There's Sickles's colt over in the medder, Jimmie," said the old man. "Don't you wish you owned one like him?"

"Um," said the boy, with a strange lack of interest. He continued his reflections. Then finally he ventured, "Grandpa—now—was that true what you was telling those men?"

"What?" asked the grandfather. "What was I telling them?"

"Oh, about your running."

"Why, yes, that was true enough, Jimmie. It was my first fight, and there was an awful lot of noise, you know."

Jimmie seemed dazed that this idol, of its own will, should so totter. His stout boyish idealism was injured.

Presently the grandfather said: "Sickles's colt is going for a drink. Don't you wish you owned Sickles's colt, Jimmie?"

The boy merely answered, "He ain't as nice as

our'n." He lapsed then into another moody silence.

—

One of the hired men, a Swede, desired to drive
to the county seat for purposes of his own. The
old man loaned a horse and an unwashed buggy.
It appeared later that one of the purposes of the
Swede was to get drunk.

After quelling some boisterous frolic of the
farm hands and boys in the garret, the old man
had that night gone peacefully to sleep, when he
was aroused by clamoring at the kitchen door. He
grabbed his trousers, and they waved out behind
as he dashed forward. He could hear the voice
of the Swede, screaming and blubbering. He
pushed the wooden button, and, as the door flew
open, the Swede, a maniac, stumbled inward,
chattering, weeping, still screaming: "De barn
fire! Fire! Fire! De barn fire! Fire! Fire! Fire!"

There was a swift and indescribable change in
the old man. His face ceased instantly to be a
face; it became a mask, a gray thing, with horror
written about the mouth and eyes. He hoarsely
shouted at the foot of the little rickety stairs, and
immediately, it seemed, there came down an
avalanche of men. No one knew that during this

time the old lady had been standing in her night clothes at the bedroom door, yelling: "What's th' matter? What's th' matter? What's th' matter?"

When they dashed toward the barn it presented to their eyes its usual appearance, solemn, rather mystic in the black night. The Swede's lantern was overturned at a point some yards in front of the barn doors. It contained a wild little conflagration of its own, and even in their excitement some of those who ran felt a gentle secondary vibration of the thrifty part of their minds at sight of this overturned lantern. Under ordinary circumstances it would have been a calamity.

But the cattle in the barn were trampling, trampling, trampling, and above this noise could be heard a humming like the song of innumerable bees. The old man hurled aside the great doors, and a yellow flame leaped out at one corner and sped and wavered frantically up the old gray wall. It was glad, terrible, this single flame, like the wild banner of deadly and triumphant foes.

The motley crowd from the garret had come with all the pails of the farm. They flung themselves upon the well. It was a leisurely old machine, long dwelling in indolence. It was in the habit of giving out water with a sort of reluctance. The men stormed at it, cursed it; but it continued to allow the buckets to be filled only after the wheezy windlass had howled many protests at the mad-handed men.

With his opened knife in his hand old Fleming himself had gone headlong into the barn, where the stifling smoke swirled with the air currents, and where could be heard in its fulness the terrible chorus of the flames, laden with tones of hate and death, a hymn of wonderful ferocity.

He flung a blanket over an old mare's head, cut the halter close to the manger, led the mare to the door, and fairly kicked her out to safety. He returned with the same blanket, and rescued one of the work horses. He took five horses out, and then came out himself, with his clothes bravely on fire. He had no whiskers, and very little hair on his head. They soused five pailfuls of water on him. His eldest son made a clean miss with the sixth pailful, because the old man had turned and was running down the decline and around to the basement of the barn, where were the stanchions of the cows. Some one noticed at the time that he ran very lamely, as if one of the frenzied horses had smashed his hip.

The cows, with their heads held in the heavy stanchions, had thrown themselves, strangled themselves, tangled themselves: done everything which the ingenuity of their exuberant fear could suggest to them.

Here, as at the well, the same thing happened to every man save one. Their hands went mad. They became incapable of everything save the power to rush into dangerous situations.

The old man released the cow nearest the door, and she, blind drunk with terror, crashed into the Swede. The Swede had been running to and fro babbling. He carried an empty milk pail, to which he clung with an unconscious, fierce enthusiasm. He shrieked like one lost as he went under the cow's hoofs, and the milk pail, rolling across the floor, made a flash of silver in the gloom.

Old Fleming took a fork, beat off the cow, and dragged the paralyzed Swede to the open air. When they had rescued all the cows save one, which had so fastened herself that she could not be moved an inch, they returned to the front of the barn and stood sadly, breathing like men who had reached the final point of human effort.

Many people had come running. Some one had even gone to the church, and now, from the distance, rang the tocsin note of the old bell. There was a long flare of crimson on the sky, which made remote people speculate as to the whereabouts of the fire.

The long flames sang their drumming chorus in voices of the heaviest bass. The wind whirled clouds of smoke and cinders into the faces of the spectators. The form of the old barn was outlined in black amid these masses of orange-hued flames.

And then came this Swede again, crying as one who is the weapon of the sinister fates. "De colts! De colts! You have forgot de colts!"

Old Fleming staggered. It was true; they had forgotten the two colts in the box stalls at the back of the barn. "Boys," he said, "I must try to get 'em out." They clamored about him then, afraid for him, afraid of what they should see. Then they talked wildly each to each. "Why, it's sure death!" "He would never get out!" "Why, it's suicide for a man to go in there!" Old Fleming stared absentmindedly at the open doors.

"The poor little things!" he said. He rushed into the barn.

When the roof fell in, a great funnel of smoke swarmed toward the sky, as if the old man's mighty spirit, released from its body—a little bottle—had swelled like the genie of fable. The smoke was tinted rose-hue from the flames, and perhaps the unutterable midnights of the universe will have no power to daunt the color of this soul.

NOTE ON THE TEXT

This edition of *The Red Badge of Courage* has been set from the first published version by D. Appleton & Co., 1895. Although several other significant texts for *The Red Badge of Courage* exist in manuscript form, contemporary scholars regard the Appleton text as the most authoritative. Typographical errors that appear in the Appleton edition have been corrected here and are listed by page and line number: 6.13, *bank;* 49.24, *would;* 54.1, *Se;* 60.6, *knitting;* 69.22, *emblem;* 82.1, *aid;* 85.12, *guilt and;* 86.25, *with a;* 96.25, *different;* 104.13, *shoulders;* 120.15, *way* [comma omitted]; 121.15, *weight like;* 140.3, *recognzied;* 143.2, *draw;* 164.4, *continued;* 166.23, *somtimes;* 170.10, *yellings;* 173.2, *burlike;* 180.18, *burs;* 182.2, *an';* 184.14, *onto;* 206.7, *illusions;* 218.12, *laughin' an'* [comma omitted]; 220.3 and 4, *major generals;* 224.8, *ups;* 232.11, *savage* [comma omitted].

COMMENTARY

GEORGE WYNDHAM

STEPHEN CRANE

H. G. WELLS

THEODORE DREISER

JOSEPH CONRAD

ERNEST HEMINGWAY

GEORGE WYNDHAM

Mr. Stephen Crane, the author of *The Red Badge of Courage* (London: Heinemann), is a great artist, with something new to say, and consequently, with a new way of saying it. His theme, indeed, is an old one, but old themes re-handled anew in the light of novel experience are the stuff out of which masterpieces are made, and in *The Red Badge of Courage* Mr. Crane has surely contrived a masterpiece. He writes of war—the ominous and alluring possibility for every man, since the heir of all the ages has won and must keep his inheritance by secular combat. The conditions of the age-long contention have changed and will change, but its certainty is coeval with progress: so long as there are things worth fighting for fighting will last, and the fashion of fighting will change under the reciprocal stresses of rival inventions. Hence its double interest of abiding necessity and ceaseless variation. Of all these variations the most marked has followed, within the memory of most of us, upon the adoption of long-range weapons of precision, and continues to develop, under our eyes, with the development of rapidity in firing. And yet, with the exception of Zola's *la Débâcle,* no considerable attempt has been made to portray war under its new conditions. The old stories are less trustworthy than ever as guides to the experiences which a man may expect in battle and to the emotions which those experiences are likely to arouse. No doubt the prime factors in the personal problem—the chances of death and mutilation—continue to be about the same. In these respects it matters little whether you are pierced by a bullet at two thousand yards or stabbed at hands' play with a dagger. We know that the most appalling death-rolls of recent campaigns have been more than equalled in ancient warfare; and, apart from history, it is clear that, unless one side runs away, neither can win save by the infliction of decisive losses. But although these personal risks continue to be essentially the same, the picturesque and emotional aspects of war are completely altered by every change in the shape and circumstance of imminent death. And these are the fit materials for literature—the things which even dull men remember with the undying imagination of poets, but which, for lack of the writer's art, they cannot communicate. The sights flashed indelibly on the retina of the eye; the sounds that after long silences suddenly cypher; the stenches that sicken in after-life at any chance allusion to decay; or, stirred by these, the storms of passions that force yells of defiance out of inarticulate clowns; the winds of fear that sweep by night along prostrate ranks, with the acceleration of trains and the noise as of a whole town waking from nightmare with stertorous, indrawn gasps—these colossal facts of the senses and the soul are the only colours in which the very image of war can be painted. . . .

Mr. Crane, for his distinction, has hit on a new device, or at least on one which has never been used before with such consistency and effect. In order to show the features of modern war, he takes a subject—a youth with a peculiar temperament, capable of exaltation and yet morbidly sensitive. Then he traces the successive impressions made on such a temperament, from minute to minute, during two days of heavy fighting. He stages the drama of war, so to speak, within the mind of one man, and then admits you as to a theatre. You may, if you please, object that his youth is unlike most other young men who serve in the ranks, and that the same events would have impressed the average man differently; but you are convinced that this man's soul is truly drawn, and that the impressions made in it are faithfully rendered. The youth's temperament is merely the medium which the artist has chosen: that it is exceptionally plastic makes but for the deeper incision of his work. It follows from Mr. Crane's method that he creates by his art even such a first-hand report of war as we seek in vain among the journals and letters of soldiers. But the book is not written in the form of an autobiography: the author narrates. He is therefore at liberty to give scenery and action, down to the slightest gestures and outward signs of inward elation or suffering, and he does this with the vigour and terseness of a master. Had he put his descriptions of scenery and his atmospheric effects, or his reports of overheard conversations, into the mouth of his youth, their very excellence would have belied all likelihood. Yet in all his descriptions and all his reports he confines himself only to such things as that youth heard and saw, and, of these, only to such as influenced his emotions. By this compromise he combines the strength and truth of a monodrama with the directness and colour of the best narrative prose.

From "A Remarkable Book," *New Review*,
January 1896

STEPHEN CRANE

[I] have only one pride—and may it be forgiven me. This single pride is that the English edition of *The Red Badge* has been received with praise by the English reviewers. Mr. George Wyndham, Under Secretary for War in the British Government, says, in an essay, that the book challenges comparison with the most vivid scenes of Tolstoi's *War and Peace* or of

Zola's *Downfall;* and the big reviews here praise it for just what I intended it to be, a psychological portrayal of fear. They all insist that I am a veteran of the civil war, whereas the fact is, as you know, I never smelled even the powder of a sham battle. I know what the psychologists say, that a fellow can't comprehend a condition that he has never experienced, and I argued that many times with the Professor. Of course, I have never been in a battle, but I believe that I got my sense of the rage of conflict on the football field, or else fighting is a hereditary instinct, and I wrote intu-itively; for the Cranes were a family of fighters in the old days, and in the Revolution every member did his duty. But be that as it may, I endeavored to express myself in the simplest and most concise way. If I failed, the fault is not mine. I have been very careful not to let any theories or pet ideas of my own creep into my work. Preaching is fatal to art in literature. I try to give to readers a slice out of life; and if there is any moral or lesson in it, I do not try to point it out. I let the reader find it for himself. The result is more satisfactory to both the reader and myself. As Emer-son said, "There should be a long logic beneath the story, but it should be kept carefully out of sight." Be-fore *The Red Badge of Courage* was published, I found it difficult to make both ends meet. The book was written during this period. It was an effort born of pain, and I believe that it was beneficial to it as a piece of literature. It seems a pity that this should be so—that art should be a child of suffering; and yet such seems to be the case. . . . Personally, I like my little book of poems, *The Black Riders,* better than I do *The Red Badge of Courage.* The reason is, I suppose, that the former is the more ambitious effort. In it I aim to give my ideas of life as a whole, so far as I know it, and the latter is a mere episode, or rather an amplification. Now that I have reached the goal, I suppose that I ought to be contented; but I am not. I was happier in the old days when I was always dreaming of the thing I have now attained. I am disappointed with success, and I am tired of abuse.

From *Stephen Crane: Letters,* edited by R. W. Stallman
and Lillian Gilkes, 1960

H. G. WELLS

[Stephen Crane's] success in England began with the *Red Badge of Courage,* which did, indeed, more completely than any other book has done for many years, take the reading public by storm. Its freshness of method, its vigor of imagination, its force of color and its essential freedom from many traditions that dominate this side of the Atlantic, came—in spite of the previous shock of Mr. Kipling—with a positive effect of impact. It was a new thing, in a new school. When one looked for sources, one thought at once of Tolstoy; but, though it was clear that Tolstoy had exerted a powerful influence upon the conception, if not the actual writing, of the book, there still remained something entirely original and novel. To a certain extent, of course, that was the new man as an individual; but, to at least an equal extent, it was the new man as a typical young American, free at last, as no generation of Americans have been free before, of any regard for English criticism, comment, or tradition, and applying to literary work the conception and theories of the cosmopolitan studio with a quite American directness and vigor. For the great influence of the studio on Crane cannot be ignored; in the persistent selection of the essential elements of an impression, in the ruthless exclusion of mere information, in the direct vigor with which the selected points are made, there is Whistler even more than there is Tolstoy in the *Red Badge of Courage*.

From "Stephen Crane from an English Standpoint,"
The North American Review, August 1900

THEODORE DREISER

It pleases me no little to learn that the Schoolmen's Club is to honor Stephen Crane with a bronze tablet. He was among the very earliest of my purely American literary admirations and one of the the few writers who stood forward intellectually and artistically at a time when this nation was as thoroughly submerged in romance and sentimentality and business as it is today. At that time, in so far as America was concerned, there were but James and Howells and Mark Twain among the elder realists and Garland and Fuller and Crane as beginners. Of this younger group Crane was a peer. And he certainly had more of a directness and force and daring than most of his elders. "Maggie" and "George's Mother," while little more than sketches in the best sense, bear all the marks of a keen and unblessed sympathy with life, as well as a high level of literary perception. . . .

The little that Crane did, as you will note, was done with fire and a conscious or unconscious independence of our strawy and smothering notions and theories in regard to letters. Also it boded well for American letters. He took our hampering hurdles without thought or a care. The "Red Badge of Courage" is a fine picture of war. And it is not pleasant. There is not much sweetness about it and very little uplift. It ends as it begins, grimly, and without any solution, moral or spiritual. This in itself is wrong, according to our moral, and hence, our spiritual standards. If you doubt it study our current books and magazines. But let that be.

From a letter to Max J. Herzberg, November 2, 1921, published in *The Michigan Daily Sunday Magazine*, November 27, 1921

JOSEPH CONRAD

One of the most enduring memories of my literary life is the sensation produced by the appearance in 1895 of Crane's "Red Badge of Courage" in a small volume belonging to Mr. Heinemann's Pioneer Series of Modern Fiction—very modern fiction at that time, and upon the whole not devoid of merit. I have an idea the series was meant to give us shocks, and as far as my recollection goes there were, to use a term made familiar to all by another war, no "duds" in that small and lively bombardment. But Crane's work detonated on the mild din of that attack on our literary sensibilities with the impact and force of a twelve-inch shell charged with a very high explosive. Unexpected it fell

amongst us; and its fall was followed by a great outcry.

Not of consternation, however. The energy of that
projectile hurt nothing and no one (such was its good
fortune), and delighted a good many. It delighted soldiers, men of letters, men in the street; it was welcomed by all lovers of personal expression as a
genuine revelation, satisfying the curiosity of a world
in which war and love have been subjects of song and
story ever since the beginning of articulate speech.

Here we had an artist, a man not of experience but
a man inspired, a seer with a gift for rendering the significant on the surface of things and with an incomparable insight into primitive emotions, who, in order
to give us the image of war, had looked profoundly
into his own breast. We welcomed him. As if the
whole vocabulary of praise had been blown up sky-
high by this missile from across the Atlantic, a rain of
words descended on our heads, words well or ill chosen, chunks of pedantic praise and warm appreciation, clever words, and words of real understanding,
platitudes, and felicities of criticism, but all as sincere
in their response as the striking piece of work which
set so many critical pens scurrying over the paper.

One of the most interesting, if not the most valuable, of printed criticisms was perhaps that of Mr.
George Wyndham, soldier, man of the world, and in
a sense a man of letters. He comes to the conclusion

that: "Mr. Crane has contrived a masterpiece." "Contrived"—that word of disparaging sound is the last word I would have used in connection with any piece of work by Stephen Crane, who in his art (as indeed in his private life) was the least "contriving" of men. But as to "masterpiece," there is no doubt that "The Red Badge of Courage" is that, if only because of the marvellous accord of the vivid impressionistic description of action on that woodland battlefield, and the imaged style of the analysis of the emotions in the inward moral struggle going on in the breast of one individual—the Young Soldier of the book, the protagonist of the monodrama presented to us in an effortless succession of graphic and coloured phrases.

• • •

This war book, so virile and so full of gentle sympathy, in which not a single declamatory sentiment defaces the genuine verbal felicity, welding analysis and description in a continuous fascination of individual style, had been hailed by the critics as the herald of a brilliant career. Crane himself very seldom alluded to it, and always with a wistful smile. Perhaps he was conscious that, like the mortally wounded Tall Soldier of his book, who, snatching at the air, staggers out into a field to meet his appointed death on the first day of battle—while the terrified Youth and the kind Tattered Soldier stand by silent, watching with awe "these ceremonies at the place of meeting"—it was his fate, too, to fall early in the fray.

From Preface to *The Red Badge of Courage* (London: William Heinemann, 1925)

ERNEST HEMINGWAY

There was no real literature of our Civil War, excepting the forgotten "Miss Ravenall's Conversion" by J. W. De Forest, until Stephen Crane wrote "The Red Badge of Courage." . . . Crane wrote it before he had ever seen any war. But he had read the contemporary accounts, had heard the old soldiers, they were not so old then, talk, and above all he had seen Matthew Brady's wonderful photographs. Creating his story out of this material he wrote that great boy's dream of war that was to be truer to how war is than any war the boy who wrote it would ever live to see. It is one of the finest books of our literature and I included it entire [in "Men at War: The Best War Stories of All Time"] because it is all as much of one piece as a great poem is.

If you want to find out how perfect a piece of writing is try to cut it for the purpose of making a selection for an anthology. I do not mean how good a thing is. There is no better writing on war than there is in Tolstoy but it is so huge and overwhelming that any amount of fights and battles can be chopped out of it and maintain all their truth and vigor and you feel no crime in the cutting. Actually "War and Peace" would be greatly improved by cutting; not by cutting the action, but by removing some of the parts where Tolstoy tampered with the truth to make it fit his conclusions. The Crane book, though, could not be cut at all. I am sure he cut it all himself as he wrote it to the exact measure of the poem it is.

From Introduction to *Men at War: The Best War Stories of All Time,* edited by Ernest Hemingway, 1942

READING GROUP GUIDE

1. The novel's famous opening paragraph ends with these words: ". . . And at night, when the stream had become of a sorrowful blackness, one could see across it the red, eyelike gleam of hostile camp fires set in the low brows of distant hills." How does this sentence set the tone for the rest of the novel? Do you find echoes of this sentence in the subsequent pages?

2. In the first paragraph is Crane's first usage of the word "red." What else in the book does he describe as red? Is his usage of the word sometimes surprising? How so? H. G. Wells refers to this as Crane's "force of color." What do you think Wells means by this?

3. Why does the narrator always refer to the protagonist as "the youth." We only learn Henry's name from his fellow soldiers; why does the author do this? How does this affect the story?

4. Henry's first encounter with a corpse both startles and numbs him. Crane describes it this way, "[Henry] vaguely desired to walk around and around the body and stare; the impulse of the living to try to

read in dead eyes the answer to the Question." What do you think the Question is? Why do you think Crane chose to capitalize this word?

5. In Chapter 3, the regiment's preparation for battle is described: "During this halt many men in the regiment began erecting tiny hills in front of them. They used stones, sticks, earth, and anything they thought might turn a bullet. Some built comparatively large ones, while others seemed content with little ones." What does this say about the different way men prepare themselves for war? Who is noticing this difference, the narrator or Henry himself? Are they the same?

6. Chapter 4 ends with, "The youth achieved one little thought in the midst of this chaos. The composite monster which had caused the other troops to flee had not then appeared. He resolved to get a view of it, and then, he thought he might very likely run better than the best of them." What does this imply? What is the monster? Why is Henry capable, or believes he is capable, of seeing it when the others are not?

7. Joseph Conrad described Stephen Crane as a man "with an incomparable insight into primitive emotions, who, in order to give us an image of war, had looked profoundly into his own breast." Why is

Crane's rendering of war so moving? How does it successfully portray the horrors of war in a little over two hundred pages, when most war novels are epic in length and scope? Why do you think Crane chose to write his novel this way?

8. Why does Henry leave his regiment? Is it an act of courage or cowardice? How does Henry perceive it himself?

9. What ultimately is Henry's red badge of courage? Is it his wound to the head, or is it something else?

A Note on the Type

The principal text of this Modern Library edition
was composed in a digitized version of
Horley Old Style, a typeface issued by
the English type foundry Monotype in 1925.
It has such distinctive features
as lightly cupped serifs and an oblique horizontal bar
on the lowercase "e."